LYNCH TOWN

Sheriff Jim Conner captured a gangling horsethief who turned out to be the nephew of the man he'd stolen the horses from, and if this didn't cause Jim Conner enough discomfort, when the lad was sentenced to be hanged, Sheriff Conner felt worse.

He found the rich rancher from whom the lad had stolen the horses was a notorious gambler and forger from Wyoming who had acquired all his wealth by cheating his nephew—the young horsethief. From then on, Sheriff Jim Conner did everything he could to prevent the hanging from taking place.

LYNCH TOWN

Lauran Paine

GUNSMOKE

First published in the UK by Hale

This hardback edition 2009
by BBC Audiobooks Ltd
by arrangement with
Golden West Literary Agency

ISBN 978 1 405 68183 4

British Library Cataloguing in Publication Data available.

Printed and bound in Great Britain by
CPI Antony Rowe, Chippenham, Wiltshire

CHAPTER ONE

THE TOWN lay in a bend of the Chagres River, and although it was obvious from the number of rangemen riding its roads and moving back and forth among its stores and saloons that Lincoln was a cow-town, it certainly had at one time been something more than that, because the town of Lincoln had brick buildings and trees, and genuine iron tie-racks, as well as other appurtenances which said Lincoln was not only an old town in Nebraska Territory, but also that it had been here, making its own way, long before cowmen took it over.

For one thing Lincoln had road lamps. For another it had a bank, a doctor, even a bakery run by a Dutchman of some kind; German, Austrian, Lowlander, it didn't make much difference. The cowboys couldn't understand him most of the time and he really wasn't vital to them in any sense, but he surely could turn out sweets, and to men whose vocation limited the intake of confectionery to a little sugar in black coffee when they could get it, the Dutchman was a real godsend. But no one took him seriously. Wherever he'd come from his culture had been as alien to the American West as the West's culture would have been in reverse. He didn't belong, and yet he added a mote to the motleyness, and actually that's what made the culture.

Lincoln's permanence was a thing folks felt. In a land where everything west of the Missouri was either bat-and-board or mud-wall construction, Lincoln's bold red brick, occasional iron railing, straight roadways and large trees down the centre of Main Street, gave an air of solid substance; of permanent survival under all adversities, natural or otherwise.

Nebraska Territory had two towns called Lincoln. That wasn't odd; Nevada had five, Arizona three, California three, and over in Illinois where Abe Lincoln had grown to manhood, there were at least seven towns called Lincoln. All that proved was that folks were almighty proud of Honest Abe Lincoln. Or perhaps it proved they simply lacked imagination.

The town of Lincoln lying in a bend of the Chagres River was surrounded by some of the best cow country on the Nebraska Plains. That other town of Lincoln wasn't much suited for cattle. The Chagres came more or less out of the north and after making innumerable dog-leg bends like the one down at Lincoln, it went meandering southward without much concern for anything, even its own willow-lined banks, for every now and then with no predictable regularity, it turned swollen and swift and sullenly poisonous like an enormous snake, flooding out of its banks and sucking away trees three and four feet through.

It never bothered Lincoln though, because there was a cut-bank bluff above the Chagres just high enough on the town side to force floodwaters to break out over the opposite, lower banks, and flood to the east.

Those floods didn't come very often though, and even when they did come, Nebraska, up in the Lincoln country alongside the river, wasn't nearly as flat as it was farther southward, so if the upper reaches got flooded, the lower plains country was a veritable morass.

Even floods didn't discourage many folk around Lincoln.

They'd been witnessing such outbreaks a mighty long time, and no matter how high the river rose and crested, nor how far off to the east the river ran and swirled like dark chocolate, there was always one of the old duffers around town who'd say, " Pshaw! You should've seen the one back in '52," or something like that.

There was scarcely an event occurred in Lincoln that one of those old mossbacks didn't belittle it, and refer to some much grander, baser, louder, taller, bigger event which occurred back in '52 or '65 or '76, or sometime. But the day they found that ragged, lice-infested band of mongrel redskins gorging on Bert Neilon's beef up in the willows on the east side of the Chagres, even the old gaffers were at a loss because, while there were hundreds of precedents involving anywhere from two to perhaps ten or twenty stolen beeves, driven off to be made sport of with arrows, then eaten, this time it was no less than a hundred head.

Another thing was the boldness of it. There those grinning tame-apes sat, stinking to high heaven, greasy, snake-eyed and as treacherous as humans could be, with a hundred head of Neilon's fattest, finest steer-critters grazing placidly around that foul-smelling camp. The redskins produced a bill-of-sale for Sheriff Conner and his bristling posse of fifty cowmen and rangeriders. They had bought the beeves in good faith, their raffish chieftain explained, paying in raw gold, and there was the paper to prove it. Their chieftain also explained that while his people didn't really like the tame taste and fat smell of white-man-buffalo, they'd decided to trade for them because they needed hides for tipis, hair for saddle-stuffing, and bones for buttons, spoons, et cetera, and the buffalo had been gone a very long time now, so they'd been reduced to living off white-man buffalo: cattle.

James Conner said the bill-of-sale had to be a forgery, but Lem Pierce, Bert Neilon's rangeboss shook his head and pronounced it genuine. That had taken the wind out of Conner. When Alfred Menard, Neilon's nearest neighbour had also studied the paper and said the signature was Bert's, Sheriff Conner stood beside his horse with the shifty-eyed Indian spokesman grinning, looking around among his uncertain possemen.

There was nothing for it but to return to town, which the possemen did, some of them baffled, some of them sullen, and some of them chiding Lem and Al Menard. " It just don't make sense, an' you got to admit that; Bert wouldn't trade off any hundred head of his best critters to a bunch of thievin' redskins."

The trouble was that Bert Neilon was at Council Bluffs on business and no one knew when he'd return. Until he *did* return there'd be no way of ascertaining whether he'd traded with those red-hided mongrels or not. By the time he eventually did return, the Indians had long since struck their camp and meandered off into the broken, wild and trackless upper reaches, heading, so it was said, into Wyoming with what remained of the cattle.

Bert fired Lem Pierce that same day he left Sheriff Conner's office, so red in the face he was on the verge of a stroke. He also cut Al Menard off the very next time they met as though Al had somehow been part of the conspiracy. Al's reaction, because he was just as tough and tempered as Bert, was to hire Lem on the same day Bert fired him, and for thirty days after that folks, particularly the townsmen and cowmen of the countryside, disputed the knotty problem. Then something happened that stopped all their speculations. Sheriff Conner went after a trio of horse-thieves operating in the cane-brake country of the northern

Chagres, and managed to sneak up on the outlaws when the first blue hint of dawn lay over the empty world, with a posse of five men, and take one of them alive.

The fight had been savage and very one-sided, but horsethieves, even ones not yet fully awake, knew they might just as well die in their soogans as submit docilely and be taken to some town where a holiday would be declared so everyone would come and watch their hanging.

There wasn't anything too extraordinary about all this. Horsethieves were common enough; in fact, of all outlaws the ones who flourished most were those who stole fast horses and rode them across endless wastes to other lands where they could make a decent profit. Hanging horsethieves was common too, but this time Jim Conner had himself a boomerang. At the cut-and-dried hearing before Lincoln's Judicial District Judge, George Meany, the local general store proprietor, the youthful, smiling horsethief who'd survived that fierce but brief gun battle, blandly told the court that he didn't feel he and his defunct friends had really been stealing horses at all. When asked why he'd made such a statement, the horsethief, whose name was Carl Overton and who'd only just begun to shave the summer before, said he and his friends had felt that way because the outfit they were raiding was owned by a man named Cody Younger, and Cody was one of the most notorious cowthieves who'd ever lived; had in fact, only a few months before gotten clean away with stealing a hundred head of prime beeves from some ranch down around Lincoln.

Since the only recent theft of a hundred head of prime critters had occurred during that interlude with the mangy redskins, everyone in that courtroom—which was the upstairs community hall above the judge's mercantile establishment—sat like stone, gazing at the prisoner. Jim Conner perhaps was one of the first to scent something big here. He leaned in his chair fingering his watch-chain, staring hard at the bold, reckless, rather handsome face of the horsethief. Judge Meany leaned down too, pressing his paunch against his table. He said, " Son; if you're makin' talk to avoid your just deserts, you're treadin' on almighty shaky ground the way you're doin' it."

Young Overton turned his clear blue glance upon fat George Meany and softly said, " Judge; you're goin' to hang me no matter what. I know that. Now tell me, in my boots, what would you do—tell a lie or tell the truth?"

Judge Meany raised his head in a sniffing way. " I'm not before the bar of justice here," he said haughtily. " You are. I've seen many just like you, boy. You figure you're a goner so you're goin' to try an' drag down some decent folk along with you. Makin' a statement like you just made with nothin' more than talk—horsethief-talk at that—to back it up, won't make this court better disposed towards you."

Carl Overton's faint smile faded. He looked across at Jim Conner, who was still staring hard at him. " Have it your way," he said, with a little toss of the shoulders. " You asked an' I told you. Cody Younger's a rich man, sure, an' he's mighty respected hereabouts, I've been told while I was in Mister Conner's jailhouse. Well folks; I know what's goin' to happen to me. I'm not dropping to my knees to you at all. I'm simply answerin' your questions the best way I can. That's a damned fact an' you can believe me or not."

The hearing didn't last much longer. Judge Meany hit his desk-top and pronounced the invariable sentence for a horsethief : " . . . An' hang by the neck until you are dead !" Then he also pronounced the rest of it. " . . . . To be taken back to the jailhouse an' there confined until the last day of this month, when you'll be taken by the sheriff o' this county to the suitable place out back o' the town, and there sentence will be carried out in conformance with law, sometime between six in the mornin' and six in the evenin', at the discretion of Sheriff Conner."

So ended the trial of Carl Overton, horsethief, sentenced to depart this earth by violence in the nineteenth summer of his life.

That didn't cause much of a stir in Lincoln where they'd been dropping rustlers of one kind or another through the community trapdoor out back of town for fifty years and better. What caused the sudden silence and deep reflection was what young Overton had said about Cody Younger. It passed over town rather as a stunning shock. In his store after the sentencing George leaned across the counter and made deprecatory sounds. " They all have to try something. There's never been a truthful horsethief born. Of course it's a ridiculous consarn lie. What did he hope to gain? A reprieve maybe; some mercy from the court. Who knows what makes those thievin' outlaws lie? No; whoever heard of anythin' so crazy; of course I don't believe a word of it. An' who'd know better? Let me tell you, strictly between us y'understand—not for publication aroun' town—but I carry Mister Younger's account here at the store and there's no better customer on the prairies. No sir. Pays up prompt, always a gentleman, an' you go ask Jim Conner—when his riders come to town no drunken brawls, no shootin' out the street lights. This Overton just tried to shock the town with that consarn pack of lies, but I tell you right now it's not goin' to do him one speck of good. Not one speck. He'll hang just like the others have done, an' for tellin' that big dirty lie before a room full of folks, I hope he dies hard."

Well. There was no other way to die dangling at the end of a twelve-foot drop, secured around the throat by a hemp rope with The Knot set just right, so it slammed savagely against a man's head beside the ear, theoretically so it would induce unconsciousness. Every hanged man who ever stood up there on the trapdoor waiting, died hard, because he died twice, once when he heard the sentence, again when he stood there looking at all the avid, twisted, knowing faces below him, waiting. He died hard all right. Maybe being in a man's nineteenth summer made it even a little harder. Jim Conner thought it did; he'd hung his share but it made him a little ill to kill those clear-eyed, downy-cheeked young ones. Some men just weren't good law-enforcement officers, it seemed like.

CHAPTER TWO

JUDGE MEANY hadn't just passed that sentence by rote. He'd known in advance of the trial or any viewing of the prisoner what his sentence would be. It was a natural thing; there was no other sentence available. So George Meany had studied his calendar. It was near the end of the month when he passed sentence. Overton had eight days left to live when Jim Conner had manacled him and herded him back to the jailhouse.

No one could accuse Judge Meany of being a production-line hanging judge. He *had* looked at his calendar. Of course he hadn't paid much attention to the criminal, and he'd had a thoroughly closed mind to anything the prisoner had to say, but nevertheless he *had* given Carl Overton eight more days of life, and that, as George Meany himself pointed out twice to Jim Conner, was a " . . . right civilised, humane act."

Well maybe. Jim didn't argue the issue, but it stuck in his head that somewhere down the line between apprehension and conviction, everyone had lost sight of the real issue, which wasn't a horsethief, nor a band of scruffy redskins, or even those valuable hundred critters. The real issue for Jim Conner was: How did Lem Pierce and Al Menard, who knew Bert Neilon's handwriting better than anyone alive, just about, make such a dramatic mistake?

Jim ambled over to the *Lincoln National Bank*, nailed Sam Avey, the manager, and asked to see some of Bert Neilon's handwriting. Sam was an agreeable, pleasant man. A bullet through the right elbow twenty years back had incapacitated him for most jobs, but not for the one he now held. He dug out letters, slips signed by Neilon for deposits and withdrawals, and lay them down upon his desk for Sheriff Conner to study.

Conner made his mental comparison. All the signatures corresponded perfectly. He sat down in a chair across from Sam and squinted his eyes nearly closed. The hell of it was that although he was positive the signatures *were* the same, he didn't have that bill-of-sale from the Indians. Without that he had nothing at all except this uneasy stirring in the back of his mind.

Sam was discreetly curious. " It's got to do with that kid you're going to hang, hasn't it?" he asked.

" Partly," conceded Sheriff Conner standing up and re-settling the hat atop his head. " Much obliged, Sam." He

walked out of the bank before Avey could put any more
questions to him. Jim Conner at thirty-four, knew the best
way to keep a secret was simply to keep it. He liked Sam
Avey. In fact, if he'd been inclined to tell anyone what was
bothering him, he'd probably have told Sam. He just
wasn't inclined to discuss it at all.

The thought haunted him for several days that if he
could find that damned redskin and get the bill-of-sale . . .
But that wasn't possible. Those Indians had probably
traded off the last of the critters for whisky, then had
scattered into the mountains of Wyoming like a covey of
quail.

But those damned signatures *had been identical*!

The third day after Overton's sentencing he rode out to
Al Menard's spread six miles northeast of Lincoln. He left
town while it was still dark in order to reach the ranch before Menard, his new rangeboss Lem Pierce, and their
riders, would be heading out for the day's work. He made
it just fine; they were all sitting down to breakfast and
Menard asked Jim Conner to join them. Jim did, and ate
like a horse even though he felt the changed atmosphere as
soon as he stepped through into the cook-shack's lampglow.
The cowhands, three in number exclusive of the *cosinero*,
the owner, and the rangeboss, had bumps of curiosity as
high as a mountain about the lawman's presence.

Afterwards, Al hung back and waited for Jim to get it
off his chest. The others reluctantly drifted on out heading
for the barn and the working-corrals. By that time the sun
was a gigantic fireball teetering upon the thin edge of the
earth's far-away horizon. Jim was conscious of the *cosinero*
gathering up dishes, cups, shuffling around with his big ears
wide open, and suggested he and Menard step outside for
their after-breakfast smoke.

Once outside Jim spoke bluntly. " Al; it's about that bill-of-sale."

Menard's brows dropped darkly. " I'm sick an' tired of that whole blasted business, Jim," he growled. " I've told it a hundred times and no one believes me. I've sold Bert Neilon cattle plenty of times, an' I've also bought animals from him. I can show you at least ten bills-of-sale with his signature on 'em. Now by gawd, Jim, I ought to know his handwritin' when I see it. The signature on that bill-of-sale was Bert Neilon's. Maybe the damned fool forgot, or maybe he was drunk, I don't know. But I *do* know that was his blasted signature. Now that's all I got to say about it. That business is beginnin' to devil me even in my sleep."

" Sure," soothed Sheriff Conner, lighting a cigarette and gazing down where the rangeboss and riders were saddling up. " Have you and Lem talked about it?"

" A dozen times, yes. An' he'd take the same oath I would. Jim, Lem's seen Bert's signature even more times than I have. He'd know it, wouldn't he?"

" I'd sure reckon so, Al."

" Well then, dammit; just answer me one thing? What's wrong with Bert anyway, firin' the best rangeboss he ever had when he knows in his doggoned heart he *did* peddle those critters to the redskins?"

Sheriff Conner couldn't answer that, and shortly afterwards he left Menard's place bound over across their adjoining ranges to Bert Neilon's headquarters-ranch. There, his reception was even more prickly. Neilon's riders were gone, only the chore-boy, the cook, and a dog half the size of a Shetland pony were in the yard when Conner rode in. The dog bayed like a wolf and Jim stepped off over at the barn tie-rack, secured his horse, and walked ahead fifteen feet between his horse and the dog, then knelt and chuckled.

That seemed to throw the dog off entirely. If Jim had stood his ground, had backed up, had even stayed prudently in his saddle, the dog would have understood all those signs of fear because he'd encountered some variation of every one of them dozens of times before. But this laughing and squatting down was a questionable thing. The dog stopped barking. With the chore-boy watching in the barn doorway, the big dog gave his tail a little tentative wag. Jim Conner grinned. The dog grinned back. Jim said softly, " You big overgrown bluff—come here," and the dog dropped its great flat head, dropped out its tongue and ambled on over to get a pat, a scratch behind the ears, and Jim Conner had made a friend.

" Dammit, Sheriff," said a testy voice from over yonder in front of Neilon's big sprawling house, " I bought that danged dog to keep watch over things. If everyone makes friends with him what good'll he be?"

Conner straightened up, the huge dog looking up at him, standing close to Conner's leg. " You could always throw a saddle on him," said Conner, and walked over to the porch where Neilon was darkly scowling. " In a pinch you could jerk the meat; I'd say from the size of him he'd feed a tribe of Indians for three, four days, Bert."

Neilon's hard blue eyes flashed straight out at Jim Conner. His brows didn't rise but an expression of thoughtful suspicion replaced the earlier look of annoyance. " You were just ridin' by," he said tartly.

" Nope. I came directly here, Bert. I just want to hear you say it one more time."

" Say what; that I didn't trade those damned cattle to the redskins?"

" Yeah. And that you haven't signed any bills-of-sale in the past month or two."

"Jim; I haven't signed a bill-of-sale in over a year an' a half. The last time was when I sold some critters to that darned cantankerous Al Menard. 'That satisfy you?'"

"Nope. Why would Lem and Al swear up an' down that was your signature, Bert?"

"Well, how the hell do I know? All I can tell you is that before I had to go down to Council Bluffs I told Lem under no circumstances to let those prime critters out of his sight. But he did. So I fired him."

"Aren't you curious about that bill-of-sale, Bert?"

"Of course I'm curious about it." Neilon dropped his eyes but didn't soften his dark scowl. In a rough voice he said quietly. "Lem was my rangeboss—my darned right hand, in fact— for five years . . ." He looked up, a sweeping, tough glance from beneath bushy, lowered brows. "I got my suspicions, Jim, but I wouldn't prosecute Lem Pierce for five times that many cattle."

Sheriff Conner stood looking at the older man. So that was it. Bert felt Lem had been involved in rustling, but since there'd always been a well-known closeness between the quiet, pleasant rangeboss and the old widower, Neilon was hiding a deep-down disappointment under the bombast, and wasn't going to do any more about it than brood and swear a little.

Jim straightened up and started to turn away. "Bert, you know a damned sight better than that," he said, and went hiking back towards his horse where the big dog was sitting, tongue out a foot, bony tail softly sweeping the ground.

"Wait a minute," called Neilon, stepping down and walking out into his sunlighted big ranchyard. "What d'you mean—I know better'n that?"

Conner strolled on, tugged loose his rein and gave the big

dog a pat on the head as he said, not even looking up,
" Lem wouldn't steal from you. He'd have let 'em cut off a
hand first. But even if he had done it—will you explain to
me how he got that bill-of-sale?"

Neilon stopped twenty feet away, glaring. He turned
Jim's question over very carefully in his mind, then he said,
" I just can't figure that part of it out, an' so help me, I've
tried."

Jim turned, toed in and rose up to settle across his saddle.
" Yet you'd fire him—just like that. Bert; I'm gettin' a little
disappointed in you. Hell; if the boot was on the other foot
I can tell you right here an' now, Lem never would have
treated you the same way."

It wasn't a very long ride back to Lincoln from the
Neilon place, and in the late springtime it was pleasant
covering that distance, but Sheriff Conner scarcely felt the
good warmth across his shoulders or on his back, and he
failed entirely to appreciate the pleasant fragrance of grass
and hot earth and green buds even when he crossed over
easterly and came to the river where he paused to water his
mount. Over there, lay a graceful kind of filigreed shade
cast by creek-willows and larger trees. They were full of
bird's nests and he was berated by several species of outraged birds for invading this greeny sanctuary.

He thought and thought and came up with a simile between himself and a squirrel in a cage. The harder he tried,
the more he was travelling in useless circles. Ordinarily
there wouldn't have been a problem; ordinarily he'd have
told himself Neilon had signed that damned bill-of-sale
then had forgotten it, or hadn't wished to acknowledge it
for some personal reason, and that would have been the end
of it, since the cattle were gone along with the redskins, and
there was no case to prosecute. Or he'd have said the bill-

of-sale had been a forgery, exactly as Bert had sworn up and down that it was, except that those mangy Indians hadn't been able to draw a straight line in the dust, let alone forge a complex signature.

And of course that led him back to something he'd been toying with ever since the trial of Carl Overton: Forgery all right, but damned *good* forgery.

He got back astride and ambled on back to town, arriving there with two-thirds of the day shot, and the remaining one-third of it thickening with sunset's long, slanting red shadows.

Old Jerry Harkness, the liveryman, took Conner's horse and sprayed runway-dust with an amber stream, hoisted his cud to the opposite cheek and said: " Jim; tell me somethin' that's puzzled me for six days now: Jest how come George Meany to sentence that young feller to a hangin' when didn't any of you find no stolen horses when you raided his camp?"

"We found the horses, Jerry. That's how come us to backtrack the thieves. He and his chums had already peddled them over near the Wyoming line."

"Then what ever possessed the young fool to traipse back down here so soon afterwards? Jim; it don't make a whale of a lot of good sense to me; I've been handlin' horses one way or another nearly fifty years, an' I've lost my share to thieves. I've even leaned m'weight on a hangrope a time or two, but this here business just doesn't somehow ring true to me."

Jim had seen old Harkness at the hearing, so he said, " You heard everything, Jerry. The boy admitted stealing those horses. What more do you figure the law should have, to make its judgement?"

Harkness screwed up his face at the sheriff. " Just tell

me this," he said, staring straight into Conner's eyes. " Do you feel easy in your conscience about hangin' this boy, Jim?"

The answer to that was simple. " I've never felt right in my conscience about hangin' anyone, Jerry. This boy or any of the others."

Sheriff Conner walked out of the barn into the late day redness. He hadn't eaten since breakfast time out at the Menard ranch, but he wasn't hungry. However, he was a little seat-weary, so he struck out up the plankwalk for his jailhouse. The moment he entered, his prisoner, over in a strap-steel cage along the exposed rear of the office, said he was famished, so Jim Conner dutifully went across to the café and fetched back a tray of beans and fried meat, black java and a tumbler of water.

Overton ate noisily and greedily. When he finished he said he was out of tobacco so Jim tossed his own sack of makings through the bars, then went to his desk and sat down, heaved his hat upon the wall-peg above, swung around and soberly contemplated his prisoner. Two more days to live . . .

" You young damned idiot," he said pleasantly. " Why didn't you take up robbing stages, or playing crooked cards?"

" Those things take skill," said the youth, softly grinning as though at some monstrous joke. " What's the matter, Sheriff; losing your nerve?"

" I sure am, son."

" Well I'm not."

CHAPTER THREE

GEORGE MEANY brought up the subject of the hanging that evening in Duane Culver's *Black Eagle Saloon*, by inquiring whether Conner had inspected the scaffold yet. Conner hadn't.

"Well why not," George wanted to know. " Jim you better get one of the carpenters aroun' town to go out there tomorrow and test things. Don't want a botched-up mess, do we?"

Conner drank his second shot of whisky and turned a baleful glance upon Meany. It was one of the facts of life that although people were supposed to respect honest, upstanding, prosperous merchants, because they successfully conformed to everything in life which was clean and decent and solid, Jim Conner didn't like George Meany.

It wasn't anything personal, exactly. In fact, Jim couldn't have defined his dislike in words if he'd tried. It was a feeling; a presentiment, a kind of wrong-scent, or something.

"Well," said George, rearing up a little at the bar and seeing the raw stare coming his way, "it's not my doings, y'know. I don't make the laws any more than you do. I've got to go by the book too, Jim. Lord knows that boy's mighty young to be dropping through a trapdoor."

"Then put it off for ten days," said Conner, signalling for a refill.

"What for? What good will that do? Listen, Jim; you heard him. He confessed to you right after you took him. You know better'n I do, even, that he's guilty."

The drink came. Conner lifted it, swallowed once, after the liquor had passed his throat, and put the glass down very gently. "For one thing," he mumbled. "Mister Younger who lost those horses we traced down and got back, didn't sign a complaint against the kid."

"*You* signed it. Cody Younger didn't have to, under those circumstances. You know that, Jim. Hell's bells, that's the law."

"All right; but I think there's something here we're all missing, somehow. I think the kid's involved in something else."

"What difference can that make? Whatever else he's mixed up in, when he drops through that trapdoor and breaks his neck, he'll pay back society for whatever else he's done, too."

Conner pushed the whisky glass away from him with a savage gesture and turned, his grey stare like dark ice. "Damn it," he snarled. "It sure must be nice to have life figured out as neat and orderly as you've got it, George. Everything fits a pattern for you. There's nothing but right an' wrong. Let's hang the kid because we've got the authority to, and to hell with whatever else could be involved." Conner paused to softly belch and drag a dark hand across his thin mouth. He hauled back off Duane Culver's bar and walked out of the saloon leaving George Meany and several others who'd heard his last words gazing after him, including the *Black Eagle Saloon's* proprietor, Duane Culver.

"Too much temper," grumped Meany, straightening forward and glaring at his own reflection in the back-bar mirror. " I've said right along Jim Conner's temper was goin' to land him in a peck of trouble some day."

Duane Culver was a burly six-footer, dark as a half-breed and quiet. No one could ever remember seeing Duane ruffled about anything, and of course there wasn't much in this little exchange to roil him, so he stood back there behind his bar eyeing George and saying nothing except that he'd always found Sheriff Conner to have a good head on his shoulders.

Meany didn't bother disputing that, he simply ordered another drink.

Outside, with dusk settling, and the sounds of people, the scent of supper-fires, the sights of Lincoln all blending together making a composite of another day's end in this town, Sheriff Conner gazed down towards his jailhouse. He'd tried drawing the condemned man out every day since Overton had been sentenced, and had gotten nowhere. Always the youth had some smart-alecky remark, and his smile.

It didn't help any, feeling sorry because the kid wasn't even twenty years old yet, and was going to die. Talking to others, such as George Meany just now inside the saloon didn't help any either.

With nothing to lose but some sleep, which didn't care about losing anyway, Conner got his horse and rode out of town heading through the settling night towards Cody Younger's spread.

Younger wasn't exactly a newcomer in the Lincoln country, but he'd only bought in four years earlier, and in the eyes of folks whose grandfathers had come here in fringed buckskin to trade with the redskins, Younger was an upstart greenhorn.

Jim Conner, who knew stockmen, had a different idea

altogether; newcomer though Younger might be, he surely wasn't a greenhorn. He'd bought out three large spreads that adjoined and had put together one of the largest cow ranches in this section of Nebraska Territory. On top of that he knew cattle; when he stocked his land he didn't buy any old gummer, cull cows, or any smooth-mouthed bulls. The same when he hired his riders. He took on only the best hands. His rangeboss was an old Montana hand named Lionel Walsh—whom everyone called Wally.

Cody Younger was a big, handsome man, florid and blunt and rough acting. He was better than six feet tall and packed a lot of rock-hard gristle. Where he came from, what the source of his wealth had been before he landed in the Lincoln country and put down his roots no one knew, and, like George Meany, as long as he bought high and paid prompt, no one much cared.

Sheriff Conner had met Younger three or four times, and if Jim hadn't cottoned to him, exactly, all that meant was that they were different enough to jangle on one another's nerves.

The same applied to Lionel Walsh, the rangeboss. He wasn't Jim Conner's type either, but cowmen who knew, said Wally was about as good a rangeboss for a big spread as they'd ever come across.

Jim knew Wally only as a careful, lanky, slit-eyed individual with a hawkish look to him; he'd struck Conner the first glimpse as a bad man to cross with guns or fists, but there'd never been anything to occur to support that notion. In fact, there were weeks at a time when neither Walsh nor Cody Younger appeared in town. Even when they did ride in, it was usually only to transact ranch business, maybe have one drink at Culver's saloon, then lope back out again.

Conner knew the minute he came onto Younger's land, now as always, because the fat cattle carried that big Y brand on their left ribs. It was so big a man could see a Big Y critter's mark long before he could even make out whether he was looking at a steer or a cow.

He was intercepted this trip, too, by Wally Walsh himself. Walsh came up out of a rocky arroyo, sat his saddle a while watching Conner approach, then loped on down to meet him. It was a perfectly natural meeting. Jim raised his hand in a loose wave and Walsh responded the same way, then swerved in to ride stirrup with Jim on the way towards the headquarters-ranch.

Jim said, " Figured you'd be at supper."

Wally had already eaten, he said, and had come back down the range looking for a sore-footed bull one of the riders had said he'd spotted. " When they're huntin' up mudholes to soak fevered feet in, they don't breed many cows. If he's too bad off we'll have to replace him." Wally eyed Conner briefly then said, " Cody's not at the home-place, if you come out to see him. But if there's anythin' I can do . . ."

Jim doubted that there was. He felt mildly disappointed and reined up. There wasn't much sense in continuing his ride if he wasn't going to find Cody at home. " It's probably just a wild goose chase anyway," he mumbled, gazing at Walsh. " I wanted to talk to him about those horses we found that the kid in my jailhouse and his dead pardners stole."

Wally stopped, looped both reins and said, " Oh. Well; we got the horses back. I reckon as far as Cody's concerned that's the end of it."

" Maybe for Cody," said Jim Conner. " But the lad hangs tomorrow."

" So I heard," murmured Wally, showing no particular concern. " Well; one less horsethief, eh, Sheriff?"

" Yeah."

Conner studied the stitching on his saddlehorn. " Nope; just wondered if getting those horses back would help me talkin' Mister Younger into goin' into town first thing in the morning to talk to Judge Meany."

" About the kid?"

" Yeah. He's only nineteen years old. I don't know how many horses he's stolen in his lifetime, but I can tell you one thing, Wally, not very many at nineteen."

Walsh's dark brows settled and his long, lipless mouth flattened slightly as he said, " Let me get this straight, Sheriff; are you sayin' you figure Cody ought to ask that storekeeper-judge down in Lincoln to let the kid off?"

" Not exactly let him off, Wally. Just get Judge Meany to give the lad another ten days."

" What good'll that do? If I was fixin' to hang, believe me I'd want to do it an' get it over with."

Jim gazed at the tough, square-jawed face and wondered. No man was anxious to die, not even a tough man. " Will you see Mister Younger tonight?" he inquired, and Wally shook his head.

" He's gone north for a few days. I don't reckon he'll even be back in the country for maybe a week. Maybe even two weeks, I can't say for sure." Wally straightened up and picked up his reins. " Sheriff; I can tell you here an' now, though, if Cody was here he wouldn't do it. He doesn't like horsethieves."

Sheriff Conner ended this talk and headed back the way he'd come. Wally rubbed him the wrong way, back there, and yet, Walsh's reaction hadn't been any different than any other cowman's reaction to leniency for a horsethief would have been. Knowing that, however, didn't change anything for Jim Conner.

When he got back to town it was late, after ten o'clock, so he left his horse at the liverybarn and strolled up to Culver's place for a nightcap. That was where he ran into Sam Avey in his shirtsleeves. They talked over a late drink the way old friends do, speaking of everything and nothing. Then Sam made an odd remark. He said for the first time in three years he had to go down and work late making out the weights and papers for a gold shipment.

" The last time we shipped gold out of Lincoln," said Sam, " was when some Arizonans passed through heading for the Missouri to buy oxen. Here; let me get the next one: Duane . . . ? Couple more . . . It's an odd thing about gold, Jim; I'll bet you outside of maybe a few real good miners and bankers, no one knows that the gold coming from different parts of the country is regionally identifiable. I mean, California gold looks one way, Wyoming gold another way, Montana gold still another way."

Jim didn't know this. He didn't actually care, right at the start of their conversation, either, then, as Sam talked on, loosened and comfortable after his second or third drink, Jim began to pay attention. Finally, when he could, he asked where this particular gold had come from Sam had to go down and weigh at the bank.

" Wyoming. I'd stake my life on it, that's how sure I am. Not just out of some worked-out old glory-hole either, down around the old ghost towns, but from some mountain stream no one's worked before. Genuine raw, virgin Wyoming mountain fine." Sam downed his drink and tossed Jim a lofty look. " I know," he said, and lightly tapped the bartop for emphasis. " No one fools me on gold, Jim."

" What's it doing 'way down here in Lincoln?" Conner asked.

" Cody Younger deposited it with me a few days back. He didn't say, an' I didn't ask, how him to come by it. That's one thing about gold, Jim. No one counterfeits it. It's either the genuine stuff or it's iron pyrites. That's all there is to it."

Jim looked long at Sam Avey, then signalled Duane for another pair of drinks. Something alarming had just popped into Jim's head. He said no more until their drinks had come and he'd paid for them. Even after that, he was careful. All he said was, " Cody must've been in Wyoming a week or two back; probably picked it up at a crap table or a poker game."

Sam shrugged. " Who knows? Maybe like you say, he won it. All I know is that it's Wyoming gold, and as sweet to see as a mother's love."

" How much of it is there, Sam?"

" Five hundred dollars worth."

Jim reached for his glass, then halted to consider the amber whisky a moment before pushing the untouched glass away. Five hundred dollars would be just about the right amount of money too, at fifty dollars a head, more or less. He hung against the bar afraid of his own thoughts.

" Hey; drink up," commanded Sam, getting fairly well oiled.

Jim nodded absently and reached for the little glass. He needed it, because those thoughts of his just didn't make good sense. Why would a rich cowman like Cody Younger peddle a hundred of someone else's fat cattle to some mangy Indians? Of course there was a very simple answer: because Cody wanted that five hundred dollars worth of gold, and because no crook worth his salt would peddle his *own* beef when someone else's even better beef was close at hand.

But right there the logic ended. Younger was a rich man. He owned more land and cattle than Jim Conner could shake a stick at. Of course Conner knew that a crooked mind just couldn't pass up even the small opportunities. That had been proven time and time again. But—Cody Younger?

He left Sam and ambled back down to the jailhouse for one last look at his prisoner. On the way he bumped into Lem Pierce, just getting astride out at the tie-rack in front of the variety, gambling house. Lem asked if Jim had seen Bert Neilon lately. Jim said that he had; he also said Bert was troubled over the firing. Lem was sanguine about that.

" He should be. For five years in sleet, snow up to my hip pockets, mud and fryin' heat. Then he thinks I'd do *that* to him."

Jim stood gazing up the lamp-lighted roadway at Lem's broad shoulders as the rangeboss loped on out of town. Strange how tough, grown men, got a deep-down liking for one another. Lem's words had been bitter, resentful, but his eyes had mirrored only hurt.

Jim crossed over and stopped outside the jailhouse to make a smoke, took down several big lungfuls, then reached for the latch and barged on in. Tonight, if he had to sit up until dawn, that damned kid was going to talk some sense and quit his everlasting bitter-sweet smiling!

CHAPTER FOUR

THE CELL was open and the kid was gone!

It was such a completely unexpected thing Jim Conner stood there in his doorway staring, smoke from that cigarette drifting up past his eyes unheeded.

He closed and barred his front entrance, crossed over with quick strides and made a careful examination. Someone had come in here with a chain-ratchet and a pry-bar. The Lord only knew how long it took him, but perhaps with the kid's aid not too long. He'd broken the door-lock.

Jim hadn't been absent too long. A couple of hours, give or take a few minutes. He left his office after blowing out the lamp, barred the door from outside and passed swiftly down to the liverybarn. The nightman was asleep, wetly snoring upon a cot in the harness room, so Conner saddled up his horse without any assistance and curved out back of town making an ever-widening circle, which would be the only way he'd catch those two since it was far too dark to pick up any fresh tracks.

By Sheriff Conner's estimate the kid and whoever had sprung that cell door couldn't be more than, at the very most, one hour ahead of him, and more probably they weren't more than half an hour or less, ahead of him. The trick, as he rode that big circle, was to listen carefully. It was a reasonable assumption two fleeing men wouldn't ride slowly when they left town, and it was that sound, in the end, which finally set Sheriff Conner on their trail. He picked up the distinct echo of two racing horses not more than a mile ahead parallel to the stageroad and bearing towards Al Menard's range.

Of course the possibility also existed that what Jim was chasing would turn out to be a pair of Menard's riders having a race on their way home, or for that matter, any pair of exuberant cowboys who'd spent a liquid evening at Culver's bar. What convinced Jim either of these possibilities were true tonight, was the simple fact that the men fleeing ahead of him didn't haul back and 'blow' their horses, but rode hard and relentlessly for nearly two hours before they even slowed a little. Desperate men rode that hard. No other horseman did.

Conner was an old hand at this game of hide-and-seek whether he played in daylight or dark. As soon as he felt a lessening of the speed on ahead, he slowed his own animal to a steady walk and let the fleeing men widen their separating distance.

He knew Overton, and Overton's rescuer, would very shortly halt altogether, listening for pursuit. They wouldn't pick up a sound because Sheriff Conner wasn't making one even though he was still advancing.

The night was particularly dark out away from town where there'd been at least some reflected lampglow to help. As far as Jim Conner was concerned the darkness was his friend while it was working against Overton, up there, and whoever that was with Overton.

As he poked along, halting often to listen, he speculated on this jail-breaker up ahead. What intrigued Jim was that Carl Overton'd had two friends when he'd come to the Lincoln country. Sheriff Conner and his five-men had shot those two to death at the horsethief-camp, so, presumably young Overton who was by his own admission a newcomer to Nebraska, had no other friends around the countryside. Yet someone, on the eve of the day before Overton was to hang, had risked his life to break Overton out of jail. There were a few folks around who didn't agree with George Meany's peremptory sentencing; not very many though, and in general the hanging of a horsethief no matter how peremptory his sentencing or how youthful he might be, wasn't the issue at all; it was his act: The stealing of a man's horse was without doubt the most heinous crime short of murder an outlaw could commit.

So it struck Jim as being rather doubtful that some bleeding-heart variety of sentimentalist, or misguided moralist, had broken the kid out of jail. And the tools he'd obviously used to wrench open the steel door weren't tools some idealistic damned fool would happen to cart along with him. Finally, that was no amateurish job back, whoever had set the ratchet-chain to use the leverage of one man to spring the door before giving it one quick, decisive spring, breaking and buckling it, knew exactly what he was doing.

Jim had no doubts about getting Overton back because regardless of how experienced his rescuer was at springing strap-steel doors he was making every novice's mistake now, when he was being pursued. And Jim wanted a good look at his rescuer. He felt almost more professional interest in the rescuer than in Carl Overton.

They had travelled a considerable distance up-country across Al Menard's range before Jim, pausing to listen, detected a slight change in the course of the fleeing men. They were angling over more towards Big Y range now. He shrugged and also altered course, but he decided now the chase had gone on about long enough, and made a more drastic alteration which would, if he were very careful, put him either alongside his prey or out front where he'd get a good chance to stop them cold.

By now they were far enough from Lincoln to be entirely alone out upon the farthest range. Whatever happened out here was going to be difficult for someone because a man could shout until his lungs burst, or even shoot a gun, and no one was going to hear and come pell-mell to the rescue.

Jim knew this country as well as he knew his name. He was familiar with each arroyo, every clump of trees, every jumble of rocks. He was also totally familiar with the distances and the gradients. It wasn't hard, therefore, to determine that if the pursued duo kept at their present course they'd come out somewhere up behind Cody Younger's home place. When he finally booted his mount over into a lope, cutting in to force a confrontation, he speculated only that his prey was heading in that direction to perhaps steal a pair of fresh horses. After all, one of them was an admitted horsethief, and the possibility was strong that Overton's rescuer might be the same.

There was an oak grove not more than a mile ahead of Jim which he made for, faded out into, stepped down with his carbine in hand, and went out to the very edge of, waiting to catch a sighting of the slow-riding escapee and his companion. He heard them coming long before he spotted them. It was a dark night making it very difficult to distinguish much more than a pair of mounted silhouettes riding slowly, at a comfortable walk, and occasionally talking in quiet, far-away voices.

Sheriff Conner shook his head. This was like shooting ducks in a rain-barrel. He raised his carbine and eased the hammer back very softly. The riders out there, southward

B

from him no more than three hundred feet, suddenly halted. Jim's breath caught in his throat. He thought they might have detected the sound of his rifle mechanism drawing taut.

But that wasn't it. One of the figures climbed down, dropped flat and pressed an ear to the ground, listening. Jim Conner's lips drooped harshly. It was a little late to be listening for hoofbeat-reverberations in the ground. He felt scorn for those two out there and guessed—correctly as it turned out—that Overton's rescuer had to be just as youthful and inexperienced as the horsethief was.

Jim ordinarily wouldn't have given any warning beyond one quick call to surrender, but patently, these were hardly worthwhile enemies. They were young and bold and—foolish—so he stepped out of his trees with the carbine held belt-buckle high and silently trod ahead until he saw the one on the ground begin to rise up, at the same time telling his companion there was no sound of anyone chasing them.

Jim let the dismounted one get up next to his horse with both hands high, one on the saddlehorn, the other hand holding the reins, the wisp of mane-hair along the horse's neck at the withers, then he very briskly said, " Don't make another move!"

Conner's words travelled like steel balls dropping on glass, bell-clear and deadly. Those two figures out there, one mounted, the other one in the act of mounting and caught in about as defenceless a position as a rangeman could be caught in, froze. Even their horses acted startled by the abrupt appearance of that armed apparition from out of the rearward grove of trees.

The one on the ground was Overton. He said, evidently recognising Sheriff Conner's voice, " All right. I don't know how you did it, Sheriff, but you win this go-round."

Jim walked on up and, made reckless perhaps by his contempt, eased down the hammer of his carbine. He had no wish to kill either one of these young fools. But that was Jim's biggest error, for young Overton, who was as tall as Jim Conner but not nearly so powerful nor experienced, suddenly whirled and lashed out with one arm, knocking the carbine aside. Then he sprang straight at Conner with a hard grunt, aiming a wild overhand blow that Jim had plenty of time to duck sideways from.

Young Carl was fast as lightning; he caught himself and whirled, striking again at the carbine barrel. That time Jim yanked the weapon clear, and, angered, ripped out a hard curse and dropped the Winchester to drop into a low crouch and let two sizzling fists sail overhead. Then he straightened up and twisted, throwing the full weight of a tough, husky body behind a blasting left hand.

He connected. Young Overton gasped and went drunkenly backwards. Jim whipped clear, keeping Overton's back and shoulders to the mounted one, in this way negating the strong possibility of young Carl's partner trying for a pistol shot at Conner. He kept the fight like that because, after that initial staggering blow, Jim had the initiative. In fact he was so sure of final victory he did something he'd never before done in a brawl; he scolded and swore at Overton all the time he was cutting in and out whittling the youth down punch by punch.

"You damned young pup. When you said you didn't know anythin' about robbing stages or playing crooked cards that wasn't the half of it. You don't even know how to keep from being caught after a jailbreak. I ought to break your consarned neck! I ought to take my belt to the pair of you!"

Overton was far out-matched but he was game. He tried to land one good punch even though his reflexes and his timing were off and he turned sluggish under the hammer-blows with which angry Jim Conner peppered him. Near the end, though, when Carl took a wide-legged stand and refused to give an inch of ground, Jim slackened off. He had to respect the lad. With blood dripping from a corner of his mouth and his head lifting heavily, Carl still swung. There wasn't a shred of force left in his blows though. He was whipped to a fare-thee-well and knew it, but he had a fighting heart, so Jim eased off, rapping him a little at will, and slapping his face open-handed. Finally, disgusted with himself, he stepped back, and measured the horrified mounted one, and dropped his right hand, brought it up with his sixgun in it, and growled coarsely.

" Get down, you over there, an' if you so much as lower your right hand I'll drop you. Now get down and walk over here!"

Overton's partner did exactly as ordered, came across and stood beside unsteady Carl. Jim gave another scornful snort. Overton's rescuer was even shorter and younger-seeming than Carl.

" Take his gun out of the holster and fling it away," said Jim, swivelling his aimed sixgun to the second one. When Carl's gun had been disposed of Jim nodded. " Now your gun—and real easy."

" I don't have a gun," said Overton's companion in a tiny voice, and Jim's angry, slitted eyes gradually opened. He let his pistol barrel droop. For ten seconds he stood like that, looking more dumbfounded than dumb before he leathered his forty-five and took two big steps closer.

" You're a girl," he said softly.

Overton's companion nodded, very clearly frightened

half to death. Jim told her to take off her hat. She did and a cascading heavy mane of wavy black hair tumbled down over both her shoulders. She didn't look to Jim Conner to be over fourteen years of age. That shook him so he stepped back and gazed from one of them to the other. A kid horsethief and someone's undersized, round and big-eyed daughter. What a hell of a catch for a grim old law-dog. He spat, pushed back his hat and savagely scratched his head.

" Overton; just what in the hell are you trying to do here—getting this little girl into trouble like you've done?"

Young Carl's hat was gone. He dabbed at the trickle of blood at the edge of his mouth and gazed hopelessly at Sheriff Conner. " She's my wife," he mumbled.

" Wife! Why; she's not more than—"

" I'm the same age as he is," said the girl. " I'm nineteen." Evidently the sound of her own voice revived some spirit, for the girl gave her head a slight, defiant lilt, and also said, " And he's my husband. A woman always stands by her husband, Sheriff, even . . . even if she's scairt to death while she's doing it."

Jim saw the soft, round chin tremble. He saw how hard she was fighting to keep her heavy, full lips steady, and he had no more to say to them for as long as it took him to make a cigarette. After he'd lighted up he remembered, and tossed the makings over to Carl. Letting out a big blue cloud and dropping his gaze to the small, muscular, perfectly proportioned girl again, Jim said, his voice completely changed, made softer now and less harsh, " Tell me; did you prise that cell door open by yourself, young lady?"

She shook her head. " No. Carl showed me how to set the chain, then he prised the door from inside the cell. Carl is very strong."

Jim flicked a look at the lanky, lean frame of Overton and checked his rejoinder to that comment about strength. Maybe, in five or ten years, Carl would be strong—if he lived that long—but right now he was a bean-pole with more than enough youthful stamina, but not very much straight physical power. Still and all . . . Jim smoked and narrowed his eyes at the girl and slowly nodded his head. If she thought her husband was a strong, clever man, that too was as it should be.

" How long you two been married?" he asked.

" A year and a half," she answered.

" And where were you all the time your husband was being tried and kept in jail?"

" Hiding out here on the range collecting the things he'd told me he'd need if he ever got put in jail."

Jim took down another deep drag off his cigarette. He felt like swearing or kicking something, or even laughing out loud.

CHAPTER FIVE

HE WAS glad for the moonless night because it enabled him to get his pair of prize catches back into Lincoln without anyone seeing him doing it. After putting the Overtons husband and wife, into the cell again, and chaining the sprung cell door, he took all three horses down to the livery-barn and there ran into an angry, erudite cowboy whose profanity was both electric and graphic. Someone, he was telling an unconcerned and sleepy-eyed nightman, had stolen his horse from the rack out front of Meany's store while he'd been up at the *Black Eagle Saloon*, and if he ever found out who'd done that he'd . . .

That was when Sheriff Conner walked in leading three horses and the cowboy's eyes widened on one horse. " That's him," he croaked, pointing a rigid arm at one of the horses. " That's m'damned horse, Sheriff; where'd you come onto them thievin' devils? I'll tear 'em limb from . . ."

" You'd better learn to tie a bowline," said Jim coldly, handing the cowboy his reins. " And if you know who owns this other one, tell him to make a better knot next time too. I had a hell of a time runnin' these two down."

He hadn't actually lied because he *had* encountered some difficulty running the pair of horses down. And he didn't really *say* those two horses had simply worked loose and run off either, although the intimation was strong enough to delude just about anyone.

He held out his own reins to the nighthawk. " Put him up," he said, referring to his own animal, " and give him some grain. He's earned it today."

Back at the jailhouse, with the roadway closed and barred, Jim hauled a chair over in front of his caged captives, straddled it and gazed in. " You complicate things," he told the creamy-skinned, short, round girl. " I reckon you know I'm supposed to hang your husband tomorrow between six in the morning and six in the evening." She nodded, holding her heavy lips pursed and tight-closed. She still didn't look over fourteen to Jim Conner, but she was clean and pretty and had eyes the colour of springtime violets. He straightened, striking the back of his chair.

" Carl; you sure put her in a hell of a spot. Jailbreakin' is good for at least three years in a penitentiary."

" Hang me," he shot right back, " just let her go."

" Where did you two get married?"

" Evanston, Wyoming. That's where I first saw her. I was ridin' for her paw in the early spring."

" Uh, huh. Carl; tell me the truth now : Do her folks know where she is right now?" Jim watched the tall youth's handsome, clear eyes, then didn't wait for an answer. " All right, son; what is the name of her paw, up there in Evanston?"

" Parker. Jeb Parker."

The girl turned swiftly, her eyes flashing a warning. " Don't tell him any more," she said quickly. " Don't you understand what he's going to do?"

Carl was puzzled. He looked from Jim Conner to his wife and back again. It took a moment, but understanding finally came. " Sheriff," Overton said in a pleading way. " Don't let her folks know. Sheriff listen; I'll tell you the whole story if you'll pass us your word you won't let 'em know."

Jim heaved a big sigh, twisted to fling his hat over atop his desk and said, " Let them know what, Carl; that she's here in jail with you?"

Overton nodded. " Sheriff; we lied to you."

Conner looked stern. " You mean you two aren't married?"

" No, not that. We're married all right. We paid the dollar fee and the preacher spliced the knot. That part's plumb legal. It's just that she's—"

" Carl!"

Both the men looked at her. She was bristling towards them. It put Jim Conner in mind of an angry puppy. He said, " Listen to me, young lady; have you any idea what a hangin' means?"

Her large liquid eyes misted. She spat at Jim, " Of course I know. But you're not going to hang my husband!"

Jim raised a broad hand. " All right. I'm not goin' to hang him. At least not today. But how the devil do you expect me to help you if you won't help me?"

She stepped closer to her gangling husband eyeing Sheriff Conner with wonder and suspicion. " What do you mean by that?" she demanded.

Jim looked at young Carl again. " All right, let's have it; what were you going to tell me?"

" She's not really nineteen. We just said that. We've told everyone that, even the landlady where I had to leave her when I threw in with those horsethieves you killed over near Cody Younger's place."

With a heavy feeling behind the belt Jim said, " How old is she?"

" Fifteen."

Jim said dryly, " I missed it by a year. I figured her to be fourteen." He looked at her, cringing in there close up to her husband, and sadly wagged his head. " Folks; at the rate you two are usin' up opportunities, this life's goin' to be all out of surprises and pleasures an' laughs before you reach nineteen."

Jim fished around for his tobacco. Carl dug out the sack and held it through the bars. Jim made a smoke in total silence, he handed back the sack and smoked, studying his prisoners. He had a way out of hanging Carl Overton all right. For jail-break he'd have to be tried again if Sheriff Conner signed another complaint. Jim's eyes darkly glistened with brief pleasure about that. Meany would be fit to be tied, and yet it had been no one else but George Meany who'd been harping that neither he nor Jim Conner made the laws, all they did was enforce them.

That much was fine. Even if George tried the kid this very day, he still couldn't pronounce a judgement in less than eight more hours, which would put the hanging off that much longer.

And there was another thing; Meany couldn't hold a trial; for instance, if the man who signed the complaint wasn't on hand to prefer his charges.

Jim stood up. This was all working out very well. If he wasn't in town tomorrow, after handing George the fresh charges, that would also be precisely what he had in mind —a ride out to Al Menard's place with the girl. Al, like George, would have a fit, but Jim didn't know of any other place to hide her. Menard was a bachelor; he ran a bachelor's cow outfit. This was going to put a terrific strain on an old friendship. But Sheriff Conner was sure Al would take her in and hide her. How could a man look at anything so young and round and frightened, if he was middle-age or better, and not feel all his tough old masculine instincts rise up in growling defence?

Conner smiled. The prisoners, watching his hard, tough features, were made more uncertain than ever by that smile. There was an awful lot the very young didn't know. Jim stood up, kicked away his chair, strode to a window and looked out. The town lay quiet and dark all around. Duane Culver's place was locked up and gloomy looking. Every hitchrack in town was empty. Down at the liverybarn a pair of lamps burnt smokily, and over at the hotel another set of night-lamps burned, but otherwise Lincoln was soundly sleeping.

He went to his desk, laboriously wrote out and signed another complaint against Carl Overton, made up an estimate of the damages done to his jailhouse by the break-out, pinned the latter paper to the former one and leaned back to carefully read both. He knew what George was going to say: 'What's the sense o' this, Jim? He's goin' to hang today anyway.' And Jim also had his prompt answer. ' George; this list of repairs at the jailhouse will take money, an' I can now file a lien against his gun and horse and whatnot, to sell them after he's hung, so's we won't have to fork out county cash.' George would snort and look vinegary and expostulate, but if Jim stood firm and gently reminded him that this was what the law required . . .

Jim stood up from his desk smiling more broadly than ever. He carefully pocketed the papers, dug a key from his vest and went over to unlock the massive steel padlock which secured the logging chain now holding the cell door closed.

" Young lady," he said pleasantly, " what's your first name?"

" Elizabeth."

" Folks call you Betty?"

She nodded as Jim unwound the chain and stepped back for her to walk out. He smiled at her. " Elizabeth's a right pretty name. Come on out."

She moved closer to her husband, bristling again. Jim sighed. Carl put an arm protectively around her. Jim eyed them a moment and beckoned to the girl. She still didn't move away from her husband.

Jim said, losing his smile, " We don't have all night. I'm going to take you out to a friend's ranch and hide you."

" Why?" she asked sceptically.

Jim's patience wore thin. " Why? Because if folks know you were involved in Carl's jailbreak they'll want to try you for a crime. That's why. Now come out of there."

Carl eyed Jim Conner carefully. " What's behind this?" he asked.

"Boy," said Sheriff Conner a trifle roughly, "you've tried my patience ever since I brought you in." He paused a moment, then continued in a milder tone. "I've figured out a legal way to get a stay of execution for you. But I don't want Betty cluttering things up, so I'm goin' to take her to a friend's ranch where she'll be safe until we work some other things out."

Carl nodded and gave his wife a gentle shove out of the cell, then he stood with both hands on the bars looking at her and she at him, while Sheriff Conner re-secured the logging chain and padlock. Then Jim took the girl out into the night with him, around into the back alley, down as far as the liverybarn, and whispered for her to wait right there until he came back with a horse.

She obeyed, but when Conner walked out leading just one horse she looked at him quizzically until he explained. "If I come riding back into town at sunup leading a riderless animal, folks might wonder. This way, we ride double, and when I come back, it won't look odd. Now get up there."

It was in the small hours with a slight chill to the night as they loped steadily away from Lincoln, heading in almost the identical direction, initially at least, that the Overtons had taken after their jail-break. Neither one of them had a word to say until Menard's dark buildings hove up low and black against a lighter sky, then Sheriff Conner explained about the ranch, and also told her she was to keep out of sight of everyone except Al Menard, the owner, and she wasn't even to tell him all she knew.

They approached the main house from around back. Jim left Betty holding the horse while he hiked around and lightly tapped on a door. An owl either in the barn loft or perched somewhere equally as high, made its mournful hoot-ing sound. Aside from that the place was as silent as the night also was. Jim rapped again, slightly harder and longer the second time.

That time he got a response; not a voice, just a pair of bare feet striking wood. One minute later Al Menard appeared in his nightshirt holding a cocked sixgun. Jim pushed Al back into the parlour and identified himself, then he stopped Menard from putting aside his sixgun to light a lamp, and explained in short, staccato sentences why he was here at this hour of the pre-dawn morning.

Al had trouble understanding; for one thing he still had cobwebs in his brain, for another he'd never before in his life heard such an outlandish request. In the third place, Al Menard, a lifelong bachelor, was flabbergasted at the thought of hiding someone's wife in his house. He started to growl a protest, then stopped and scratched his awry hair and squinted his eyes nearly closed to demand if Jim Conner had been drinking.

"I haven't been drinking," exclaimed Sheriff Conner, then launched into a full explanation starting with the jailbreak and ending up with the statement that Betty Overton was standing out back of the house holding Conner's horse and waiting.

Menard went to a chair and sat down. He immediately jumped up clutching the knee-length nightshirt he was wearing. "Ya damned idiot," he roared, and fled back into his bedroom.

Jim returned to the night, went around and brought his horse and Betty to the front of the house where he made his mount fast at the tie-pole, then took Betty on into the dark parlour to await Menard's second entrance. When Al returned he was dressed, but instead of combing his hair he'd pulled his hat down low. Jim made the introductions and

Al warily eyed the diminutive young girl. He rolled his eyes back to Sheriff Conner with an expression of pure murder in the look.

"Are you absolutely sure you know what you're doing?" he demanded. "Jim; friendship's one thing. Something like this . . . well . . . you realise what you're askin'; I could get in trouble up to my withers doing something as crazy as this. Why; that girl don't look old enough to have a husband. If you ask me she don't look old enough to be *weaned*!"

Betty said, "I'm married and if I can't hide here I'll just go back with Sheriff Conner. I don't care if they try me too. If they're going to hang Carl then I don't want to—"

"Whoa now," sputtered Menard, seeing the swift scald of unshed tears and reacting just as Sheriff Conner had privately predicted. "Just settle down, missy. I didn't say you couldn't stay here." Menard shot another savage glare at Conner. "Of course I'll put you up. It's just that this here is a ranch of menfolk, you see, and—"

"My father and brothers have a man's ranch in Wyoming, Mister Menard. My mother died when I was three years old. Anyway; except for you I won't let the others see me."

The violet eyes and uncertain lips were working on Al. He swallowed and nodded, a little mournfully Jim Conner thought, then he offered a weak smile and said, "Sure, missy, sure. You just wait until I see Sheriff Conner off then I'll come back and show you which room you can have."

Menard took Jim's arm in a savage grip and left the house with Conner. He was careful to close the door before he started swearing. Jim went out to his horse, woodenly got aboard and nodded. "I'll be back in a day or two. You take care of her, hear?"

Menard shook an outraged fist in the direction Sheriff Conner rode away in.

CHAPTER SIX

IT WAS just beginning to turn light over along the eastern horizon when Sheriff Conner stepped down at the livery-barn, put up the horse he'd borrowed, and afterwards sauntered over to the hotel where he roomed, and made himself presentable for a new day as though he'd had a genuine night's sleep, which he hadn't had at all, and which he now began to miss.

Eating a big breakfast though, helped, and afterwards he went over to take a tray to Carl in his cell and to report that Betty was perfectly safe. After that, with some papers in one fist, he strolled over to Meany's mercantile establishment, catching George just as he was stoking up a fire in a wood stove to set the coffee pot on. Jim handed George the papers, leaned upon a counter and awaited the explosion. It came precisely as Jim had anticipated.

"You mean that danged horsethief escaped last night?" Meany howled. "By golly he could've cut someone's throat, Jim."

"He just wanted to get away. I went after him. It wasn't much of a chore, George. I've already told you he's just a kid. Catching someone like him is child's play."

"Well," muttered Meany, scanning the second slip of paper. "What's all this?"

"Damage to the jailhouse. He broke out using a ratchet-chain and a pinch-bar. Broke my cell door. If we file a lien we can sell his effects after the hanging for about half as much as it'll take to—"

"Doggone it, Jim; what are you talkin' about? That boy's to hang today between sunup an' sunset. If you file these darned papers it'll call for a stay of execution, and I just don't see the sense of it. Hang him, damn it. Forget the cost to the door."

"What," exclaimed Sheriff Conner, throwing Judge Meany a cold look, "and use tax money when we don't have to? George; if the folks who voted you into office heard you say that they'd never vote for you again as long as—"

"Jim!" replied the paunchy merchant waving the papers in his hand as though they were signals of some kind. "What's the sense o' all this, he's goin' to hang anyway?"

"It happens to be the law," said Sheriff Conner straightening up off the counter. "And as you said the other night up at Duane's bar, we don't make the laws, we simply enforce them." He pointed at the papers in Meany's hand. "Jailbreak, resistin' an officer of the law in the official pursuit o' his duty, flight to escape prosecution . . . George; you can't just close your eyes to those things. There's the complaint duly made out by me and signed. Overton will have to be tried again. You know that, doggone it all, *that's the law*!"

Meany put down the papers and studied Sheriff Conner's tough, craggy features a long time before he said in a very soft and suspicious tone of voice, "You're up to something. You've bit me off over sentencing that kid right from the day I did it."

" All I asked was a stay of execution."

" And this," said Meany, tapping the papers, " is your way of making sure you get it, isn't it, Jim?"

Conner gravely nodded without speaking a word. " Try him," he said. " That's the law," and started walking out of the store.

Meany lumbered after him and caught Conner just over his threshold. " Jim; I'll convene the court in two hours. By golly you're not goin' to mock me—an' the law—like this. I'll convene court in two hours and hear the charges an' pass sentence all before two this afternoon. That'll still leave you four cussed hours to hang that damned horsethief. Put *that* in your pipe and smoke it!" Meany wheeled about and stormed back inside his store.

Jim ambled up to Duane Culver's place, handed swarthy, close-mouthed Culver the key to the jailhouse padlock and asked Duane to see that his prisoner was fed at noon. He then went strolling on down to the liverybarn, hired a horse which belonged to the establishment because he felt he had used his own animal hard enough the past twenty-four hours, and he loped out of town in the clear, good warmth of a fresh day, heading for the Chagres River upstream a couple of miles where he knew of an ideal spot to nap on leaves and moss completely hidden by willows.

It had certainly been a long, interesting night, the day before, but still, a man needed his rest to be fresh enough to competently discharge his legal duties as sheriff of a county. No one could say otherwise, including a boiling-mad George Meany sitting all alone upstairs over his store, waiting for a complainant and a prisoner to appear, who just weren't going to show up.

And he slept too, for several hours with the soft-lapping water making his rest deep and wonderfully pleasant. But when he awakened a troubling thought nagged at him. Cody Younger and that Wyoming gold.

He lay for another long hour, or until the sun was close to setting, which would be about six o'clock, then he got up, caught the drowsing livery animal and slowly began to ride back towards town through soft-saffron shadows and with a benign little warm breeze at his back. He had two telegrams to send, both to Wyoming. All he had to do was avoid George Meany until he got that done, then he wouldn't care; let George get apoplectic.

But it wasn't Meany entirely, Sheriff Conner discovered the moment he circled around town and entered the livery-barn from the west, the whole town was alive with curiosity and interest. There had been a hanging slated for this day and no hanging had taken place. Of course most of the really inquisitive people had run down Judge Meany to get the straight of it, but most of the others were spreading all manner of wild rumours. Even old Jerry Harkness, the liveryman, had a story of plotting and counter-plotting to pass along to Jim Conner, even before he remembered that Sheriff Conner was official executioner for the county as well as law enforcement officer and coroner. Then Jerry spat amber, hoisted his sagging britches, and asked what really had happened to delay things.

Jim told him calmly that young Overton still had another hearing to face before he could be hanged, and went across the road to the telegraph office, got off his two wires, one to Jeb Parker at Evanston, Wyoming, the other to Wyoming's U.S. Marshal at Cheyenne.

After that he discreetly took the back alley up to the *Black Eagle Saloon*, entered through the rear door and sauntered out front where at least two dozen gossiping cowmen and townsmen saw him and stopped their talking to follow his every move with their eyes. He signalled for a drink from Duane. Culver brought it, leaned over the bar to hand Jim back his key to the jailhouse, and said in a lowered voice full of gravity, " George's been raisin' hell all over town lookin' for you. He's madder'n a hornet."

" He'll get over it," said Sheriff Conner, coolly downed his drink, paid for it, thanked Duane for looking after his prisoner, and strolled out of the saloon. At once all those humming voices started up again, only louder now than before.

Down at the jailhouse, when Jim walked in, Carl Overton blinked and sprang up off his cot. " The judge's been in here ten times since noon," he reported. " He's mad enough at you to chew nails and spit rust."

Conner didn't comment. He tossed aside his hat, dragged over the chair and sank down on it outside Overton's cell. " Betty is safe," he stated, calmly eyeing the younger man. " And now by gawd you're goin' to start at the beginning and tell me your whole story, Carl. If you don't, after I worked this hard to save your scruffy neck, I'm goin' to come in there with you, lock the door behind me, and give you all the thrashings your paw should've given you the past fifteen years, all rolled up into one. Now start talking !"

Young Overton's mouth was puffy on the left side and he had a purple bruise under one eye. He had a smoke between his fingers which he gingerly drew on, then slouched back and sank down on the pallet again, refusing to look out at Sheriff Conner.

" There's nothing much to tell. I worked for Betty's paw an' we got married. An'—"

" The horse stealing," prompted Jim.

" Oh that. Well; I met those fellers over the Nebraska

line in Wyoming. I couldn't get a job. Betty and I'd been eatin' tinned beans for two weeks. They said they could use me, so I trailed along. But I had to leave her back there. I gave her my watch and everythin' else to keep her going until I came back with my share of the money." Finally, Carl looked from beneath dark brows at Jim Conner. " She followed me. I don't know how she did it. She's sure some girl, Sheriff."

" Yeah, I know. Now tell me—who did you know down here?"

" Know? I didn't . . . Yes I did. I knew someone. An uncle. He's all the kin I had. My folks been dead since I was twelve. Epidemic carried them off."

" Who is this uncle?"

" I don't think I got to tell you that."

Jim leaned across the back of his chair, his face closed down and harsh. " Boy; you're building up to a whipping. Just one more time : *Who is that uncle*?"

" Cody Younger."

Jim's surprise wasn't perhaps as great as it might have been. " I figured . . ." he muttered, leaning back. " Get on with it."

" No. I've told you all you got to know."

Jim didn't show anger this time. He said, " All right, Carl. Then *I'll* tell *you*. Even a greenhorn horsethief doesn't come straight back and hit the same ranch twice unless he knows damned well it's safe to do so. That's what's been sticking in my craw ever since I caught you. Those fellers you met in Wyoming—you told them who your uncle was, didn't you?"

Carl nodded.

" And they knew the spread down here, so they took you in with them thinking that if anything went wrong you'd get your uncle to save their necks while he was also saving yours."

"They didn't say that," grumbled young Overton.

Jim sighed with mature resignation and eyed the younger man with asperity. "Carl; you're young and green, but you sure as hell aren't dumb. You knew that's why they took you along. Tell me something; what kind of a man do you figure to grow up into, sellin' out your own kin?"

As though impelled up off the pallet by a coiled spring, Carl whipped upright, spinning to lunge at the bars and grip them until his knuckles were white. "I'll tell you the kind of man I figure to grow up into, Sheriff. Not the kind that'd steal from a twelve-year-old kid, then leave the country without even takin' him along, after he'd cashed everything the kid's folks had left him. Not that kind by a damned sight!"

The boy's eyes were slitted and fiery, he was breathing hard, the knuckles strained even tighter on the cell straps. Jim sat in quiet thought until someone thrust open the road-side door and stamped in out of the brightness. He turned. George Meany was standing back there as red as a beet with both hands fisted on his thick hips.

"Where in the hell have you been?" snarled Meany. "Jim; you did this deliberately today. I want to tell you I won't stand—"

"Get out, George," said Jim in a low, grating voice, arising and heading across the room. "Come back an hour from now, or even later. Right now I've got other things to iron out." He reached for Meany's elbow, turned the store-keeper and gave him a hard shove out of the office. He then closed the door and slammed down the bar behind it. Outside, Meany hammered on the door and cursed. Finally he stamped angrily away.

Jim resumed his seat out front of the cell. Carl was appraising him with calculating young eyes. He showed a little more respect for Conner now, too, for as soon as Jim was seated he said, " Sheriff; that fellow wants to hang me the worst way. How come you to be against me hangin'?"

Jim thought of the big violet eyes and the trembling, round chin of Betty Overton and cleared his throat before he answered. " I just don't like hanging folks. Now back to your uncle. Are you sayin' your folks left you a ranch or something and Younger took it?"

" That's exactly what I'm saying. He was my court-appointed guardian. Now you understand why I laughed at your court, at that fat storekeeper-judge, and even at your badge? It was men like that who let my uncle clean me out in Wyoming. Then he gave me a job as chore-boy on my own ranch, after he moved in. But when he sold out and headed for Nebraska he didn't even remember to tell me he'd sold the place. That's why I came after the horses. An' I'd have kept comin' too, until I'd rustled him blind. Only you caught me."

Jim thought back to his few meetings with Cody Younger. The rich rancher had always been slightly patronising, as though Sheriff Conner were some kind of inferior two-legged critter. He shoved long legs out, crossed them at the ankles and said, " Carl; what did your uncle do for a living before he got hold of your property up north?"

" Do? Everyone knew what Cody Younger was up where we hailed from, Sheriff. He was a professional gambler, a two-bit commission dealer in cattle, a feller who lured folks into investin' in his schemes, then he'd go south with the money. You name it; my big, rich, fancy-dressin' Uncle Cody has been it, or done it, includin' robbin' me blind."

" You got my tobacco sack," said Sheriff Conner, putting

forth a hand through the bars. Afterwards, manufacturing a smoke he said, "Was your uncle ever mixed up in any shady cattle deals, Carl?"

Overton shrugged. "I don't know. All I heard about him was from eavesdroppin'. When folks knew I was around they wouldn't say anything. But one time Betty's paw and older brother were in the barn while I was forkin' hay in a corral outside; they didn't know I could hear 'em. Jeb—that's Mister Parker, Betty's paw—was mad enough to explode. I heard him tell her brother—that's Frank, the oldest one—that if he ever laid eyes on Cody Younger again he'd kill him on sight."

Jim waited, but Carl lapsed into a brooding silence. "What was that about?" he prompted the younger man. "What else did Mister Parker say?"

"Well; he said Uncle Cody had fleeced him good on a couple hundred head of cattle some way. He didn't tell Frank all the details. All I heard Mister Parker say was that anyone who was that good at forgin' another man's signature had ought to be shot."

Jim Conner sat a long while in silence, then slowly got up and went after his hat. He then left the office.

CHAPTER SEVEN

GEORGE MEANY was shocked. In fact what Sheriff Conner had just explained to him was so astonishing George was even jarred out of his earlier anger. He listened to the entire story though, and finally said that he didn't believe a word of it; that this Overton had just made it up to maybe save his neck or get another delay in his execution.

That was when Jim told Meany to remain right where he was at his office in the store, and sometime before George's supper time he'd return. Then Conner went down to the telegraph office.

One of his telegrams had been answered. It was the one from the Parkers up at Evanston, Betty's kinfolk. It said simply that whatever their girl had done was all right with them and they'd be coming on the coaches to make certain no one bothered her.

That was fine, but it wasn't the telegram Sheriff Conner wanted right at the moment. He went outside and loafed along the front of the telegraph building. Later, when it still hadn't arrived, he headed on up to the *Black Eagle Saloon*. After that, with the day nearly gone, he went down to check on his prisoner, fetched Carl some grub from the cafe, and returned to the telegraph office again. That time the reply was there; it had in fact only just arrived.

Jim read it, strolled up towards Meany's store re-reading it, and walked on into the store, down into George's back-room office, and wordlessly held out the telegram. Meany adjusted his spectacles with great care, spread the telegram upon his roll-top desk and bent to study it with as much care as though it had been the ancient map of a hidden treasure. When he was finished George handed back the telegram, removed his glasses and began to look worried.

" It didn't mention him robbin' the kid," he said weakly.

" He did that within the law, George, not outside it. He was the kid's guardian. Evidently the kid's paw didn't know his brother-in-law as well as he thought he did. Anyway," Jim waved the telegram in his hand, "how about the rest of it?"

"I don't know what to say," muttered Meany getting heavily to his feet and pacing once up and once down, his office. "He pays his bills before the tenth of each month, buys big when he comes to town, and—"

Sheriff Conner snorted softly. "All those things prove is that he just doesn't figure you're important enough to fleece." He got up, stuffed the telegram into a pocket and started for the door. "I'm going over to make out a warrant then I'm goin' out to Big Y and take him into custody."

Meany was upset. "You can't do that. Listen, Jim; you know the old saying about making haste slowly. Well; it sure fits this case. Anyway; what'd you charge him with; he hasn't broke any laws hereabouts an' if Wyoming wants him they got to wire us a hold-order, don't they? I mean, Jim, he's a big man with a big crew of riders, and we make a mistake—I mean if you make a mistake—it's going to make us look awful bad."

Those fluttery protests were still lingering in the air when Sheriff Conner left the store and hiked on across to his jailhouse to make out the warrant for arrest on Cody Younger. When he walked in he got a surprise; Al Menard was sitting there comfortably with his hat on the back of his head talking to Carl Overton. They seemed easy and confident with each other.

Jim sat down over at his desk and turned his back on Carl to ask Al if by any chance he'd seen Bert Neilon in town. Al nodded, stating that Bert was up at the *Black Eagle* with his riders, having a few beers. Also, Menard volunteered the information that he'd left Lem Pierce back at the ranch. Then Al said, "You know, Jim, that little lady can cook? Who'd ever thought anyone that young could really cook? I was just tellin' Carl here, it's been ten years since we had a gen-u-wine roast cooked with the juice still in the meat, but by golly that little gal did it neat as a pin."

Jim was pleased and said as much, although his thoughts were elsewhere. He asked if the other men knew Betty was on the ranch, and saw immediately in Al's face that they did. "But," said Menard, raising a finger in caution. "All they know is that she's the wife of a friend of mine. They don't know the friend is this here horsethief."

Jim nodded in an absent sort of way, dug around in his desk for some forms, then went to work filling out one of them; a warrant for the arrest of Cody Younger. Where he came to the space allocated for specifics, he had to pause and think. He couldn't use the forgery, or the theft of Neilon's cattle which Cody had sold to those Wyoming Indians, because there was no proof. Without proof no crime could be properly levied against a man.

As for robbing his dead sister's orphan, Carl Overton, there wasn't even a legal crime there. Moral crime, yes, and ethical crime, but not legal crime. Jim chewed his pencil thinking how much better off the world would be if justice prevailed instead of law.

As for the Wyoming charges, they weren't really charges at all. They were simply a recitation of crimes for which Wyoming had at one time or another investigated Cody Younger, or else they were crimes for which he had been briefly locked up, fined, or run out of some particular county.

Jim leaned back watching his prisoner and Al Menard amiably talking in soft tones so as not to disturb Jim, over in front of the strap-steel cell. There was no charge he could nail Younger on! He kept watching those two over across the room thinking there had to be some way he could get at Cody Younger, at the same time realising that there wasn't.

If he'd only had enough presence of mind to take that bill-of-sale from the Indian! He reached for his hat, shoved the uncompleted warrant into a desk drawer, and left Carl and Al behind in the jailhouse while he strolled up through the pleasant evening.

Out front of the stage office he met Sam Avey without a necktie and without a coat, which was unusual. Sam was lighting a cigar. He offered Conner one and got a refusal. " I like them," the sheriff explained to Avey, " but they don't like me."

Sam tilted his head to trickle out some smoke. " Finally got rid of that damned gold," he said jerking his head rearward to indicate he'd left it with the stage people to be transported southward. " Always sell the stuff to the nearest U.S. mint," he explained. " This time I sent it down to San Francisco."

" How about Younger's receipt?" asked Jim idly, thinking of the source of that gold, actually, not its destination.

Sam patted a pocket. " Got it right here," he answered, then threw a quick, sharp look at Sheriff Conner. " Say, you don't happen to be going out towards Big Y by any chance, do you?"

Conner started to shake his head. He'd planned on going to bed this night at least, at a decent hour. He said, " Why?"

" Well; the Lord knows when I'll get out that way, and since Mister Younger doesn't come to town very often, I just thought . . ."

"As a matter of fact," said Jim, "I'm on my way out there right now. At least close by."

Avey fished out a carefully folded slip of paper and passed it over. "I'm right obliged," he said, and went hiking up the dusky-lighted, shadowy roadway humming to himself around his big cigar.

Jim stood a moment considering the receipt in his hands, then thoughtfully turned and ambled on down to the liverybarn, got his horse and left town, as he usually did, by riding due west until he was clear of the roadways, then swinging northward for the big range country.

There was a curved little dagger of a moon up there for a change, and although it added to the fullness of the heavens it did not actually contribute much light. Not that Jim needed any; if there was a prairie-dog hole within twenty miles of Lincoln he didn't know about it was only because the prairie-dog had just moved in.

He hadn't, at the time he snapped up the chance to visit Cody Younger's place on legitimate business, had any idea why he wanted to go out there, since he didn't have his warrant, except perhaps a powerful curiosity. The last time he hadn't gotten very close before he'd been intercepted by hawk-faced Lionel Walsh. This time he'd get all the way to the house because no one knew he was coming, and it was too dark and too late in the night for anyone to be riding Big Y range. At least that's how he reasoned, riding down the gloomy world of Menard's range, heading towards the juncture of Al's land and the Big Y range.

What *really* ate him was what Younger had done to Carl Overton. *That* was his real motivation and he made no secret of it to himself, although he hadn't—and wouldn't—mention it to anyone else.

What kind of a man stole from a little kid, then turned

him out in a man's world where the best he could even hope for was the most menial kind of jobs, such as chore-boy on ranches, when the kid had been his own sister's youngster? It took a lot of thought, sometimes, to come up with a reason why some folks had been born, why they'd been permitted to live so long, and why they were as they are.

He fell to thinking about lanky Carl and diminutive Betty. There was something kind of pathetic in their bewilderment as they tried to rear back and face life. A horse-thief! Of all the stupid things to start out being, even when a man thought he had as good a reason for being one as young Overton thought he had.

Anything, practically, would be better than stealing horses for a living. And yet Jim Conner could understand: Being a chore-boy until he got enough experience to be a full-fledged cowboy didn't pay enough to keep a kid's body and soul stuck together. With a wife . . . Jim gave his head a hard shake. It was immature for them to be married; neither of them were old enough to understand what marriage demanded of folks. Then he got to thinking of the way little Betty had stood up to her full defiant height, which wasn't very tall, when he'd started scolding them back at the jailhouse, and he chuckled to himself in the night. Maybe he was wrong about that; maybe they *were* old enough. One thing was a lead-pipe cinch; folks had to start somewhere, so maybe getting married even before they'd worn out their teens was as good a place as any.

James Conner had never been married. He'd never even come close to being married. He only knew second-hand what marriage was all about, and yet being an older man, he had a certain wisdom, a kind of earthy intuition about those things which made him feel more than those kids could know. And one thing Jim had been through plenty of, was life. Coupled with what he suspected about marriage, this added up to experience.

He fell to speculating too, about Betty's reaction to seeing her father in Lincoln. She'd specifically asked Jim Conner not to tell her parents where she was. Carl had made that same appeal.

Now, riding along slouched and easy in the bland night, Jim's conscience hooked him a little. In retrospect, it didn't now look like he'd had to wire Jeb Parker up in Evanston after all. In fact, it began to look as though he shouldn't have done it. He gave his shoulders a little toss; a man does, usually, what he thinks is best at the time, and right then, when he'd gone out to send those two telegrams to Wyoming, he'd felt someone ought to be down here who'd be on the side of the Overtons.

What worried him a little was the prospect of Betty's father arriving here, snatching up his daughter and heading back for Wyoming with her, full of indignation, leaving Carl behind in Jim Conner's jailhouse. There was no way of accounting for the sometimes irrational and fiercely protective instinct of a parent.

Well, he told himself with resignation, that wasn't going to happen if he had to cross tempers with this Jeb Parker, and that only made him feel all the meaner, because if it happened that way Jim Conner would only have one person to blame—Jim Conner.

He breasted a rolling rib of land with several white-oaks on it and halted to make a long sweep of the onward range. Big Y's wagon-road lay on his right, but it also lay far behind him. He'd angled across Al's range so as to short-cut a lot of Big Y land and reach the vicinity of Cody Younger's home-ranch without wasting a whole lot of time. It wasn't really very late, but by the time he reached the ranch and scouted it up, then rode on it, it would be past the bedtime of most rangemen.

Not that this bothered Jim particularly; he had the darkness on his side exactly as it'd also been his ally when he'd run down and captured the Overtons. But after delivering the receipt he had no idea at all what he'd do. In fact, while he sat there gazing around, he had no clear idea of just exactly what had prompted him to ride out here in the first place, unless it was to get a real close-up look at Cody Younger.

Somewhere ahead he heard a man cry out. Then another one hooted in the watery starlight and Jim heard riders pushing a band of racing horses up-country towards the corrals of the home-ranch. He sat, speculating about that. Not many men worked after supper, and no one—with one exception—tried herding horses in a big herd in the dark. That one exception of course was horsethieves.

He eased down out of his white-oaks and made for the yonder range at a slow and careful gait. Eventually he saw orange squares on ahead, small and obscured by distance, and still farther along he picked up the dust-scent of horses.

If Big Y was running in a remuda of fresh mounts it sure went about doing it the hard way. The chances of corralling all those horses on a dark night were about as certain as whistling up a storm.

He rode on through the dust, the sounds of those racing riders growing always smaller dead ahead. It mystified him; on his own ranch Cody Younger and Wally Walsh wouldn't be rustling horses, and it couldn't be horsethieves from somewhere else because they wouldn't be driving the herd straight for the yonder lights.

He picked up his own animal and dropped him down in

a slow lope. At least he now had a reason for being there; he could say he'd been passing through, heard the horses, and had ridden over to investigate, seeing as how it was highly unusual for rangemen to be rounding up horses in the darkness.

Of course that didn't sound too substantial, and yet it was now true because he was loping along in the wake of those horses and riders full of honest curiosity.

When he came close enough to make out the buildings he heard the men shouting back and forth louder and more frequently as they corralled their catch. They'd done it after all, he reflected, which proved they were top hands.

CHAPTER EIGHT

HE WAS about a thousand yards from the yard when, his thoughts on the strange events of the night ahead and the large, handsome man who owned this big ranch, he failed to hear the hiss and sweep until it was too late and a lariat settled neatly over his shoulders. As soon, though, as that rope drew up, he stopped his horse and hurled himself off on the right side. Of course that astonished the horse, who was white-man broke not Indian-broke, and accepted riders on and off only the left side, so the horse shied violently to the left as Jim went off on the right side.

A man grunted, evidently jumping hard to tear Sheriff

Conner out of the saddle, but there was too much slack so the man stumbled where the rope should have sung taut in his hands. He stumbled and fell on all fours and cursed as he whipped half around to jump back to his feet again.

Sheriff Conner saw all this from where he lay, swiftly tearing off the noose and casting it away. The cowboy was no more than fifty feet away and jumping up again, still with the turk's-head end of his lariat in both hands. The darkness prevented him from seeing that his rope was no longer around the victim squirming out there on the dark ground.

Jim got to one knee and raised his sixgun. " Stand still," he said evenly. " You make one move and I'll kill you !"

The cowboy turned to stone, gazing with disbelief over at the blue-black, unmistakable brightness of a polished steel sixgun barrel. He let his lariat slip out of both hands.

Jim got to his feet. On ahead in the yard someone laughed long and loud over by the network of corrals. Another voice, deep and hard, called for a lamp to be brought over to the corrals. No one up there in the yonder yard seemed the least concerned that something not at all interesting or funny was occurring out a thousand yards.

Jim walked up close and urged the cowboy to turn his back to Conner. When the cowboy obeyed, Jim disarmed him, then holstered his own weapon and said, " All right, mister, you can turn back now." He gazed at the dark, half-breed face in front of him. The Big Y cowboy wasn't a tall nor heavy man, but he had that peculiar stringiness and feline poise that equalled the shattering power of sturdier builds. He would be as fast as greased lightning. From the look of his slightly tilted stone-black eyes, he would also be very dangerous as an enemy.

C

" What was the idea?" asked Jim. He'd seen this man in town a time or two; didn't know his name, but then he'd never had any reason to inquire.

" I didn't know it was you," said the 'breed, nodding at Jim's badge.

" Is that Mister Younger's idea of how to welcome folks to Big Y?"

The 'breed looked off to his right which was the direction the other men had gone with the horseflesh remuda. " We've been keepin' a right sharp watch since them horsethieves hit us last month," the 'breed explained, swinging back to face Jim Conner again. " All I know is that I'm bringin' in the drag when I hear someone comin' behind me."

" It could've been one of the others."

" No. No; they were all ahead of me. I knew that because I'd seen 'em race past." The 'breed licked his lips, looked to his right again, then said, " If you want we can walk on up there and see Mister Younger, Sheriff."

Jim nodded. " *I'll* go see Mister Younger," he said. " *You* go hunt up my horse and fetch him over to the corrals."

Jim walked away. Except for being startled half out of his boots by that lariat settling down out of nowhere across his shoulders, and a few bruises, which were accepted occupational hazards, Jim Conner wasn't bad off. In fact, as he walked ahead, towards the dusty corrals beating off dust with his hat, he considered himself lucky. If that damned 'breed hadn't swung his rope before he'd thrown it, which made that hissing sound and warned Jim at the eleventh fraction of a second what was happening, he could have wound up with a broken arm, leg, or worse.

By the time he got close enough to the corrals to see what

was going on, though, he was over being shaken up, and had made himself more or less presentable again. There were four men at the corrals. Two of them were inside and the fourth man was perched upon a log stringer pointing out which horses he wanted shunted into an adjoining corral. It all looked perfectly normal—a rancher was selecting the best horses out of a remuda—except that it was being at close to midnight of a mighty gloomy night.

Sheriff Conner had seen Cody Younger before. In fact he'd had a brief conversation with the large, youngish man a time or two down in town. But he'd never before had occasion to search Younger out, so now he walked on up from one side, slowly, and made a careful assessment of what he saw, before the big man perched on his corral-stringer-seat happened to glance around and down, and saw the sheriff standing less than fifteen feet away, looking up at him.

Evidently Younger was startled. His face didn't show it; he'd clearly schooled himself against letting his face show anything he didn't want it to show. But the slight lifting, tensing of the shoulders, the abrupt falter in Younger's mood, both told Jim he had been perhaps the farthest thing from Cody Younger's thoughts.

Younger was a handsome man although his lips were too thick and too soft. He was better than six feet tall and as flat-muscled as a youth of twenty. He had to be in his forties somewhere, but barring the deep-scored little crow's-feet wrinkles at the outer edge of each eye and the sprinkling of grey above each ear, he looked in that poor light to be much younger.

He dressed well and wore a tied-down forty-five with clean ivory handles. When he unwound and dropped to the ground facing Jim Conner, he had a slightly hostile expression down around his mouth, and a cold, speculating look to his eyes.

" You must've dropped from the sky," he said to Sheriff Conner. " I didn't see anyone ride up."

Jim wryly smiled. " I didn't exactly ride up. Some 'breed cowboy who works for you roped me off my horse back a little ways. I took his gun away from him and told him to hunt up my horse and fetch it back here." Jim reached down, drew forth the 'breed's sixgun and held it out, butt-first.

Younger took the weapon and his gaze darkened slightly towards Jim Conner, but it was impossible to say whether this change of expression meant he was sizing up the lawman, or whether he was impressed with what Jim had done to his cowboy.

" Well," he said, dropping the gun to his side. " What can I do for you, Sheriff? It's a might late for social calls, isn't it?"

" I was ridin' by and heard horsemen running a band of animals, so I came on up to look for myself. Kind of odd time to be bringing in a remuda isn't it, Mister Younger?"

The handsome, large man gazed at Jim Conner with a hint of loose indulgence on his face. " The boys forgot to get in a fresh band, and I just got back from up north this afternoon, so we decided to do it tonight. Yeah it's unusual, Sheriff, but it worked out all right. The horses knew where they were being driven and went right on in." Younger stepped closer to the corral to peek through. He sang out and gestured. Jim Conner caught a glimpse of Wally in there with another man on foot, heading for the particular animal their employer had designated was to be cut out into the adjoining corral.

Younger watched a moment longer, his back to Conner,

then he wig-wagged with both hands that the job was satisfactory, and turned back. "What'd you figure," he asked indifferently, "that I was bein' hit for by horse-thieves again?"

"It could have been that way, Mister Younger."

"I reckon it could have, Sheriff." Younger drew up his lips in a superior smile. "That other one hung yet?"

Jim kept studying the handsome, well-fed, cold and calculating face across from him. "No, not yet."

"Wally tells me you were out here a day or so back askin' if I'd ride in and tell Meany to go easy on that thief."

"That's right," acknowledged Jim, still studying that handsome, cold set of features across from him, whose smile was as false and lacking in warmth as another man's curses might have been.

"Hang him, Sheriff," exclaimed Younger, not smiling now. "I've got no use for horsethieves. Hang him and pull him up plenty high."

Jim didn't believe Cody Younger had no knowledge of the identity of the horsethief, but just to make certain he said, "He's just a kid. Claims he's nineteen but I'd mouth him at closer to seventeen or eighteen, Mister Younger. His name's Carl Overton, but that's all he'd tell me."

Younger showed nothing, not even the depths of his flinty eyes. "The sooner you hang a horsethief the better off you are, any time and anywhere." Younger fished inside his long coat for a cigar which he calmly lit and sucked on. "Why is he so closed up, Sheriff; usually horsethieves talk a leg off you to gain a little time."

Conner rested a thick arm upon a corral stringer, his eyes steady on the other man. "Not this one. He wouldn't even tell me his name until I weaseled it out of him. But I figure a kid like that can't have stolen horses before, and maybe with half a chance he'd turn into a worthwhile man."

"Not a chance in the world," growled Cody Younger. "Once a thief always a thief."

You ought to know thought Jim Conner, and looked over inside the corral to keep Younger from seeing the expression he couldn't quite hide. He fished inside a pocket and brought forth the receipt Sam Avey had given him. "By the way, before I forget it, the banker in town asked me to drop this off if I was over your way."

Younger took the paper, unfolded it, studied it up close in the bad light, then stuffed it into his pocket eyeing Jim Conner closely. Probably because he thought Jim had read the receipt anyway, he said, "I pick up a little fine gold every now and then on my business trips up into the north country. Five hundred dollars worth this time." He blew out a big cloud of fragrant smoke. "Five hundred's hardly worth fooling around for these days, but when a man doesn't have to work very hard for it, he might as well fetch it along, eh, Sheriff?"

"Yeah," murmured Jim dryly. "I've never gotten any money I didn't have to work hard for, Mister Younger." He pointed into the adjoining corral where the chosen horses were milling. "You gettin' ready to make a cattle drive?"

Younger looked around and back again. "No; it's too early yet for that. Just got a little trade goin' on some horses up north. Some Indians I know. Not much of a deal but a man likes to keep his hand in." Younger stepped back as his men opened the far corral gate to release the unwanted horses. "We've got a pot of java on the stove in the bunk-house," he said carelessly. "You're welcome to a cup if you like."

Conner turned, shaking his head. " No; thanks all the same. I was up last night so I'll just head on back and catch a little shut-eye. See you again, Mister Younger."

" Sure," said the cowman breezily, and stood watching as Sheriff Conner walked over to the tie-rack in front of the barn where his horse stood tied. Then Younger turned without another word or glance and headed on over where his riders were hiking dustily and profanely towards their lighted log bunkhouse.

The ride back for Sheriff Conner was uneventful until he began speculating on that bunch of redskins Younger was rounding up those horses for. If, by some wild accident, it just happened to be that same band Younger had traded Bert Neilon's cattle to, Jim just might run into a little luck —providing the spokesman for those savages still had that bill-of-sale. He was half afraid to speculate about that. Indians were notoriously indifferent to the white man's pieces of ' talking paper '—paper with writing on it.

Of course, if that same spokesman appeared in the county again, Jim could haul him in and lock him up as a material witness to the cattle theft, but frontier juries were notorious for their disbelief of anything an Indian said, under oath or without an oath. The sad part of this was that for a hundred years and longer, jurymen, lawmen, everyday stockmen and merchants and settlers, had known what glib and habitual liars Indians were. Especially did they lie when they thought that otherwise they might get into trouble with the law.

But that spokesman would remember where he'd butchered or sold Bert's cattle. Each of those critters had been branded. Jim wagged his head. Those blasted hides could be strung out from here to Canada.

He stopped thinking about Neilon's cattle and turned

back to trying to puzzle out what made a man like Cody Younger tick. Of course Younger had recognised the horse-thief's name, but he'd woodenly urged the youth be hung, and right away at that. His own nephew!

Lincoln showed ahead, quiet in the mid-week shadows, functionally square and tree-lined, with the river below and behind it. Years back when he'd first run for the job of county sheriff Jim Conner had thought it would be a fine thing to serve this community until he retired, and after that to sit back and maybe take life easy. He still felt that way, too, because he'd done nothing right up until now which could come back later on and haunt him. But this business of hanging Carl Overton was already haunting him and he hadn't even yanked on the rope yet.

Something else bothered him deep-down too: Cody Younger; his habit of half sneering at a man when he spoke to him, his way of sizing up folks then deliberately turning his back on them, when all the time he was blacker at heart than the meanest drunk cowboy spoiling for a fight at Culver's bar.

He rode down the far side of town, put up his horse and ambled back to the jailhouse. When he walked in, there were three stalwart, grey-eyed men standing lined up in front of Carl Overton's cell looking belligerently in. Carl was backed off and pale. His eyes flicked to Sheriff Conner with a burst of enormous relief.

Jim closed the door, set his heavy shoulders to it and forgot everything but the rawboned three men across the room who turned and gazed stonily at him.

" I'm Jeb Parker," said the greyest of the three. " These here are my sons, Frank—eldest—and John—my youngest."

CHAPTER NINE

JIM CONNER was a fair judge of men, and those three with their tied-down guns, faded pants and sweat-stained Stetsons, looked to be about as rough-tough a trio as a man might stumble onto any place Jim Conner knew of from the Mississippi west to the Sacramento.

"You made right good time," he said to Jeb Parker, after acknowledging Frank and John with a curt nod to each son.

"Took the coaches the same hour we got that telegram," explained the vinegary, grey-eyed older man, staring hard at Sheriff Conner. "Stayed aboard 'em day an' night to get here in time."

Jim tossed down his hat, dropped into the chair at his desk and raised an eyebrow, "In time for what, Mister Parker?"

"For whatever these damned Nebraskans are fixin' to do to my girl," growled the gruff, ham-handed and work-toughened older man. "Where is she, Sheriff? All we got out of that whelp in his cage was that you'd took care of her."

Jim swung the chair fully around and ran a slow, frosty glance up and down each of his three visitors. These were tough, capable men, there was no question about that, but all the same Jim Conner hadn't been a suckling too long himself. "The lad's name is Carl," he said quietly, boring

Jeb Parker with his eyes. " He's your son-in-law. Not many
fathers-in-law would call their sons-in-law whelps, even if
they didn't approve of 'em, just out of common decency for
their own daughter's feelings."

For a while a heavy silence hung in the office while Jeb
and his two lanky, rawboned, iron-like sons studied Jim
Conner. Then the eldest son, Frank Parker, said, " Sheriff;
he stole Betty and took her off with him."

" They're legally married," said Conner, not too sure
this was the truth.

Frank nodded. " We know. We found the preacher—
and ran him out of the country for that. He's lucky we
didn't hang his hide on the barn door."

" She's under age," rapped out Jeb fiercely. " She's
barely dry behind the ears."

Sheriff Conner looked at the youngest one, John. He
stood quietly by, evidently willing to back up his father and
brother in whatever happened here, and yet Sheriff Conner,
gazing into John's face, got the feeling this one was
different.

" How do you feel about it?" Jim asked.

The youngest son's dark violet eyes, very like his sister's
eyes and evidently bequeathed the clan through their dead
mother, because Jeb's eyes were flint-grey in colour, and so
were the eyes of Frank, fell upon Jim Conner with a quiet,
confident steadiness. John may have been the youngest and
therefore the least experienced, but he definitely was his
own man.

He said, " The marriage was legal. Carl's got himself
into a bushel of trouble down here, stealin' some feller's
horses, but if my sister wants him, then it's all right with—"

" Boy," snarled Jeb, glaring. " You let *me* do the talkin'
in this."

John didn't flinch but he indifferently nodded at his father, and said no more. He stepped to a little chair and eased down upon it. He wasn't an easy man to ruffle, Conner noticed, and liked the youngest Parker then and there.

" We're here to take Betty home," said Jeb. " Now where is she, Sheriff?"

Jim gazed at the ceiling a moment organising his answer to that, then he said, " Mister Parker; I think the law figures a man an' his wife make their own decisions once they're spliced. If Betty wants to go with you, I reckon Carl won't stand in her way. But if she *doesn't* want to go . . ." Jim stood up and looked at each of them in turn. " Why then I'm the one who'll stand behind her."

Jeb's neck swelled but Frank lay a hand lightly upon his father's arm and said, " Sheriff; let us talk to her."

Jim nodded. He couldn't prevent them from doing that even if he'd wanted to, and since he now understood where Betty Overton got her fire and defiance, he smiled inward at what he was positive she'd tell her father and brothers.

" Come around in the morning," he told the Parkers. " I'll take you out where she's staying. Meanwhile; we've got a fair hotel across the road and north a few doors." He went to the roadway door and held it open.

The Parkers looked at one another. They'd had their say, Sheriff Conner'd had his say. Nothing was likely to change before morning, so they all trooped out into the night and Jim closed the door after them, gazing across gravely at young Carl.

" Nice, friendly family you married into. That's the first time I ever saw three rattlesnakes coiled to strike, wearin' Stetson hats."

Carl made a feeble smile and sat on the edge of his bunk inside the cell. He said, " Sheriff; I sure was holding my breath. I expected you to say my uncle's name. That would've put Jeb right up the wall in a red froth."

Jim walked over. " You didn't tell him?" he asked, slightly curious. When the youth shook his head Jim leaned on the bars gazing in at him. " Why not?"

" They were mad enough as it was. When they stormed through that door I thought they were goin' to keep right on comin' through the bars. They were mad, Sheriff."

" Looks like they get that way right easy. All except the youngest one—John."

Carl turned his reply to that over a few times before he said it aloud. " When you get to know Jeb, he's really not like that. I know. He took me in when I didn't even have an extra pair of socks. He works a man hard, but he pays you for it, and when you make mistakes—of which I sure made my share—he'd sometimes just sort of slap you across the shoulders . . ."

Jim kept watching through the bars. When Carl let his words trail off and sat moodily looking at the floor, Jim said, " Sure. Right up until you packed off his daughter." He turned and went after his hat. It was late, he hadn't gotten his rest the night before, and although he'd napped up the river, he was still weary, so he stepped into the open doorway and said, " Well; I got a feeling when I take those Parkers out to the ranch in the morning, Betty'll yank the slack out of them, so if I were you I wouldn't worry too much."

He passed outside, closed and locked the door from there, pocketed the key and struck out straight for his room at the hotel. He had no clear notion of just exactly how he might exploit the Parkers' rancour towards Cody Younger, but he had all night and probably all of tomorrow also, to puzzle through that.

"Hey! Hey Sheriff!"

He turned with a resigned sigh. Bert Neilon and George Meany were bearing down on him from the direction of the *Black Eagle Saloon*. He stepped back out to the edge of the plankwalk and swore under his breath. Either one of those men alone was bad enough, but together . . .

"Jim," exclaimed Meany, halting under the overhang a few feet away, "Bert's got an idea that some rough-lookin' strangers who hit town today on the stage are kin of the horsethief's. He an' I been talkin' on that, an' we figure they're probably here to bust him out of your jailhouse."

Just for a second Jim's eyes narrowed, then he suspiciously said, "How many of these rough-looking men were there?"

"Three," stated Neilon. "They came in on the coach, headed for Duane's bar, bought a bottle and took it off into a corner where they sat and drank for nearly half an hour before they walked up and down the roadway sizing up the jailhouse."

"One grey, tough looking older man and a couple of equally as tough looking, rawboned younger men?"

Neilon nodded. George also bobbed his head up and down. They waited for Sheriff Conner to say something. He didn't utter a sound because he now saw himself enmeshed in his own tangled web. If he told Meany and Neilon who the Parkers were, George at least would want to know why the sheriff hadn't told him Overton had a wife. Worse yet, Meany, who was no fool, would begin to wonder about something else which he'd so far totally overlooked: How did Carl Overton get that ratchet-chain and pinch-bar he had broken out of jail with? From there it

was just one indrawn breath before Meany would say Jim
had to also arrest and confine Overton's wife as an acces-
sory.

" What are you looking like that for?" Meany inquired.
" You don't happen to know those strangers do you Jim?"

" I've seen them," admitted Conner, starting to move towards the hotel door again. " They couldn't get Overton
out of the jailhouse if they wanted to, and as far as I know,
boys, they're just three cowmen passing through. Overton
told me he has no friends around here. I don't think that's
changed any the past couple of days."

" All right," put in Neilon, conceding to Conner in this
instance. " But what about those two other horsethieves you
an' the posse killed, taking young Overton?"

" What about them?"

" These strangers could be their brothers or something.
Jim I'll tell you one thing for damned sure; those three are
loaded and primed for trouble. I know the look. I've seen it
a thousand times in my lifetime."

" In the morning," said Sheriff Conner. " If those men
hit town today on the stage they'll need sleep tonight, just
like I also need it."

He left Meany and Neilon standing out there in the
night and went on up to his room. There were times, he
told himself as he let himself into the room and reached for
the lamp, when the difference between being a peace officer
in a cow county and being a wet-nurse to all the overgrown
children who shaved and operated ranches or general
stores, was one and the same cussed job.

He bedded down with the window open above the main
roadway and the soft sounds and scents of his town coming
up to him. One thing was certain; by this time tomorrow or
much earlier, the Parkers would hear about Big Y and the

rich cowman named Cody Younger, who owned it.

He slept on that discouraging thought and awakened with it. He had no reservations at all about the Parkers salivating Cody Younger, but he kept thinking to himself that there had to be a better way to utilise their animosity towards Younger.

The answer hit him hard while he was shaving. He wouldn't need that other forged bill-of-sale if he could induce Jeb Parker to produce his equally as forged bill-of-sale. His hopes plummeted. Of course, that bill-of-sale would be up at the Parker ranch in Wyoming.

All right; but he could still use Parker and perhaps his sons to identify Cody Younger as a notorious character from Wyoming. That would be enough, especially if Jeb would sign a complaint, for Jim to go back out there and formally arrest Younger.

He finished dressing and headed downstairs for the café and breakfast. He expected to find the Parkers there but they weren't around, so he hastily ate and went down to the jailhouse. They weren't around there either. With a sinking heart he looked up and down the roadway. There was no sign of anyone even remotely resembling the three Parkers. Then a soft voice said at his back from between two adjoining buildings, " Sheriff; we got your horse rigged out in the alleyway, along with a trio of rented livery critters for us. We're ready to ride any time you are."

It was the youngest one; the long-legged, square-shouldered one named John. Jim turned and thought a moment, then said, " John; go fetch your paw. I'd like a little word with him before we pull out."

John dutifully disappeared down through the dog-trot, and moments later Jeb appeared, his face twisted with scepticism and strong suspicion. " What is it?" he demanded, and stepped up close as he added: "Sheriff; I don't like bein' horsed around."

"We have that much in common," said Conner, stifling the irritation this older man invariably sparked to life in him every time they met. "Would you sign a warrant for the arrest of a man named Cody Younger?"

Jeb Parker's face smoothed out very quickly, almost as though he were just recovering from having someone fling a bucket of cold water over him. "Cody Younger, y'say? You got a feller hereabouts by that name?"

Jim Conner stood watching the older man, saying nothing. He didn't have to answer the questions, Jeb Parker was only making conversation until he got over the shock of discovery.

Eventually, when the Wyoming rancher settled back into his normal pattern of talking and thinking, he said, "Never mind the complaint, Sheriff. Just tell me where I can find Mister Cody Younger. You won't need a warrant after we find him. All I ever heard up in Wyoming was that he'd left the country. Someone said he'd told folks he was going to Montana. Another time it was Idaho."

"It's Nebraska," stated Conner, "but I want him alive, not dead, so either you do it my way or you don't get in on it at all."

Parker looked up the road for a moment, his flinty gaze inward and thoughtful. After a while he nodded his head just once and looked back at Jim. "Fair enough. But Sheriff; if the law sets him loose, believe me he won't see a whole lot of sunsets after that."

"He stole some cattle from you," stated Jim. "That's your affair, or the affair of some Wyoming lawman. What I need is that forged bill-of-sale."

"I don't have that," exclaimed the cowman. "The feller

who bought those cattle with my mark on 'em got that bill-of-sale. I tried every way short of shootin' someone to get those cattle back. All I got was a warnin' from the U.S. Marshal that if I made trouble over what looked perfectly legal to him, he'd come after me with a troop of cavalry. Sheriff Conner; that man wrote my signature so good even my own sons could scarcely believe I didn't write it."

" Come on inside," said Jim, fishing for his jailhouse key. " I've got a complaint for you to sign."

John and Frank Parker appeared in the dog-trot looking impatient. Their father beckoned to them. " Come along boys," he called. " We're in better luck comin' down here than we knew."

CHAPTER TEN

AFTER JEB PARKER had signed the complaint against Younger and had explained to his sons that their prime enemy was in the vicinity of Lincoln, Jim Conner went with the trio around back where their horses patiently waited, then led the Parkers out of town northerly.

As they sped along, though, Jim told the boys what he'd also told their father. " You do this my way, or you turn back right now. I want Younger alive."

" Why?" asked Frank Parker. " Why would anyone want that whelp alive?"

" He wants to try him in a law-court," opined Frank's

father. " Mostly, that's how lawmen work. Catch fellers and haul 'em into court so the whole blessed community's got to chip in and stand the expense. Our way is a two-cent bullet; no arguin', no delay, no big expense."

" And no certainty you've even got the right man, either," said Jim. " Or that killing him won't work hardship on someone else."

The Parkers did not argue this point. Conner hadn't expected them to; they were dogged, blind-stubborn men, with the possible exception of young John, who'd made their minds up about life and living and dying a long time back and refused now to be confused by facts.

" How far is this ranch?" asked Jeb softly, savouring the fragrant new day.

" Not too far," Sheriff Conner told him.

" An' after we get Betty we'll ride on to Cody's place; isn't that right, Sheriff?"

" Right as rain, Mister Parker."

He led them in a slightly roundabout way. He was fairly certain Al would be at the ranch even though it was a mite late in the morning for still hanging around. But on the offchance that Al had ridden out with his men, Conner made his roundabout ride up and down and across Menard's range so if Al was out there somewhere he'd surely see Jim Conner and the three strangers heading for his ranch-yard, and lope right on in.

As it turned out the precaution was an oblique blessing; Al wasn't out with his men, he was shoeing a horse down at the barn where he first spotted horsemen coming, but his cowboys saw those four riders heading towards the home place, and recognising none of them—the distance was too great—as well as being a little uneasy, they broke off their work to turn and slowly ride along in their wake. Jim

Conner didn't know this until he'd been in the yard for several minutes. The same also applied to the Parkers. They didn't know it either until it was forcibly brought to their attention.

Jim led them straight into the yard. When Al stepped into the barn's broad doorway looking out, Jim spied him and angled on over. Al removed his hat, mopped off sweat, replaced the hat and stepped outside nodding to Sheriff Conner and the Parkers as they all four halted at his barn tie-pole.

" Al," explained Conner, " These are Betty's paw and two brothers from—"

Over at the main-house the porch door slammed. The men all turned. Betty was coming across the yard with a wadded up apron in her hands. She had her raven's-wing hair caught into a high-up pony-tail and her cheeks were flushed by the oven heat. A light streak of flour was upon one side of her face.

Jim stepped down, smiling. Jeb and the boys also got down. But if anyone expected a warm, quavering greeting, he got a rude surprise. She walked around them all and went over to stand beside Al. Her brothers grinned broadly and Jeb said, " Elizabeth, you little cuss. You sure had us worried. By all rights I ought to take m'belt to you, but I'm so glad to see—"

" Paw," she broke in fiercely, showing that same erect defiance to her brothers and father that she'd once shown Jim Conner, " I know why you're here: To take me home. Well, Paw; I'm not going! I'm a married woman now and I've got responsibilities. On top of that I *like* it down here in Nebraska. Carl and I've got plans to someday—"

" Girl," barked old Jeb, his smile withering. " You don't know what you're sayin'. You're too young to know. Furthermore; as for that damned whelp back there in the jailhouse—"

Sheriff Conner reached out and tapped Jeb's shoulder. The two men exchanged a look. Jeb turned back to his daughter.

"That *boy* in the jailhouse turned out to be nothing but a common horsethief. There's nothing lower than a horse-thief, daughter, an' we'll not have you associatin' with one!"

"She's married to one," said Al Menard, looking Jeb straight in the eye and leaning relaxed upon his barn tie-rack. "Mister; just how do you take a man's wife from him? This here little lady *belongs* to that boy in the jailhouse."

Frank stiffened in hostility towards Al. "Mister; you better keep your long nose out of this. It's a family matter."

Menard slowly shook his head from side to side. "No it's not, young feller. It's this little lady's affair, an' if she says she's stickin' by her man, why I reckon her friends got a right to back her play."

Frank eyed Al carefully, up and down. Al had been shoeing a horse, his shell-belt and pistol were hanging on a nail in the barn. "Well now," said Frank softly, "We know exactly how to handle folks who butt in where they're not wanted, Mister Menard."

Al didn't move an inch. He gazed at all three Parkers then said in an almost patronising tone of voice, "Boys; turn and look across the yard behind you." Menard's cowboys were slouching over there, looking, listening, and ready for trouble.

Jim Conner turned but no one else did. Evidently the Parkers either thought it was a ruse, or they didn't want to take their eyes off Menard. Sheriff Conner said, "Mister

Parker; those are Menard's riders behind you. I reckon they followed us on in from the range."

Jeb's nostrils flared but otherwise he showed nothing at all. His daughter said, " Paw," in a soft, little-girl voice. " I thought you'd help." It was as much a reproach as it was a small sad sound of disappointment.

For the first time the youngest Parker spoke out. John said, " Don't fret, sis, we'll help. As far as Carl's concerned; we'll help there too."

Frank turned and gazed at his younger brother while Jim Conner watched them both with solid interest. Frank was tough and older and scarred; Jim thought young John had to have grit to face this older one. But John's eyes never once wavered as he and his older brother stared at one another.

Jim finally broke the strained silence by saying: " Boys; in my county we sort of believe a wife's got rights and responsibilities. Rights to stand for what she believes in and responsibilities to her man. I reckon Elizabeth's let you know how she feels. It's not just me who's going to back her up. Not Al Menard and his cowboys over there across the yard. It's Nebraska law." He caught Jeb's gaze and held it. " Now you've seen her. I brought you here like I said I'd do. So maybe we'd better get on to the next chore we've got to look after today. You ready to ride?"

Jeb slowly turned away and glanced at his youngest son.

" You're just like your sister," he growled. " And she's as stubborn as your maw used to be. Plain bull-headed, the pair of you."

Frank said something that made old Jeb's eyes widen. " There's something here, Paw. These men are *for* her, not against her. Now how come so many of 'em can be thinkin' wrong?" Frank softly shook his head at his father.

"Maybe they aren't. Maybe it's us who are thinkin' wrong." Frank turned and looked at his sister for a moment before he said, in the same quiet, grave tone of voice. "Well hell, Paw; she may not be as old as we figure a married woman ought to be, but at least she *is* his wife."

Jim Conner raised a hand to the lower portion of his face to hide the small smile there. He and Al Menard exchanged a look neither of them saying a word. Over across the yard where Menard's cowboys were slouching, there was a noticeable loosening.

Menard said, addressing Sheriff Conner. "Where you bound for, Jim?"

"Big Y."

Menard nodded, not the least surprised. "I figured it might be," he muttered, and rummaged in a trouser pocket, brought forth a crumpled, weathered slip of paper and held it out. "I also figure Younger had something to do with this."

Sheriff Conner took the paper, looked hard at it, and stopped breathing for a full five seconds. It was the bill-of-sale that redskin had grinningly shown him when he'd asked about the Neilon cattle. "Where'd you get this, Al?"

Menard was casual. "Found it over at our calving ground. Some Indians camped there for a few days with their cattle, Jim. As usual, they tossed aside everything and left a mess at their campsite like redskins always do. See how one corner's charred? That was used to start a fire, only the paper was too wet with dew to burn so they kicked it aside and used something else."

Jim held the paper towards Jeb. Parker took it, held up close and studied it, then he said something fierce under his breath and glared as he handed the paper back again. "I'll bet this Bert Neilon whose signature is at the bottom of that damned paper no more signed that thing than the man in the moon."

Menard's brows raised a notch towards Jeb. Parker saw and said in a harsh growl. " Forgery, Mister Menard. Cody Younger done the same damned thing to me up in Wyoming. It cost me some of the best steers I had, too. I'd have killed him, but he skipped the country."

Al nodded. " That's what I figured it had to be," he told Sheriff Conner. " When I saw the signature and remember how mad Bert was, I figured it had to be forgery. But Jim; so help me when I showed it to Lem Pierce he swore up and down it was Bert's signature the same as we felt about it that other time. The notion of someone bein' able to sign another man's name so perfect he couldn't even be sure he hadn't signed it himself, just never occurred to either one of us."

Jim understood. He said, " Who else have you shown this to?"

" No one. We only found it a couple of days back. But I did figure I might ride over to Bert's place when I finished shoein' my horse with the thing."

Jim held the precious paper lightly and speculated a little. For what he proposed to do over at Big Y he really didn't need the forged bill-of-sale. He already had his warrant for arrest and his signed complaint, so he could bring Younger in. On the other hand, this was the only real piece of evidence there was to prove how, and what, Younger had done. If anything happened to that bill-of-sale, George Meany just might refuse to even hear the charge against Younger.

" Listen to me, Al," he finally said, handing over the bill-of-sale. " You go ahead and take it over and tell Bert what happened. But if you lose that piece of paper, or if

Younger or any of his hardcase cowboys get hold of it, I'll tell you right now there's not much chance of a conviction against Cody. You understand how valuable that paper is, now?"

Al took the paper and gently folded it as he nodded his head. "Don't worry; Cody Younger's the last man who's goin' to get his hooks on this, Jim." Menard straightened back and looked around. "You Parkers goin' to leave the little lady alone, or do I have to put my riders to guardin' the place against you? I'd like your word one way or another, because if you'll leave her alone, I'd like to take my men over to Neilon's with me. I don't expect any trouble over there, but I reckon Bert'll want to join with me in comin' back over to Big Y, in case Sheriff Conner needs a little backin' over there. Cody Younger doesn't hire anything but the toughest and best top-hands."

John Parker said quietly, "Betty's perfectly safe, Mister Menard. We wouldn't harm her anyway; she's our kin. All my paw and brother wanted to do was talk her into comin' back home with us." John gazed at his sister with a hint of a smile in his violet eyes. "I get the impression they failed. If she insists on stayin' here—we'll abide by that."

Jeb and Frank slowly turned and slowly considered young John. But when Jim Conner expected one or the other of them to explode, nothing like that happened.

Al nodded, accepting John's pronouncement as gospel, and called across to Lem Pierce and his other men. "Mount up, boys. As soon as I get saddled we'll head for the Neilon place."

Betty ducked under the tie-rack and went up to her father. "You be careful," she said swiftly. "Paw; please don't be mad. He's—my husband."

Jim Conner saw the liquid mist in her large violet eyes

and switched his attention to her father. Old Jeb's thin lips loosened, his rough right hand came up to gently lie upon her shoulder. He said in a soft-gruff way, " I ought to take you over my knee is what I ought to do, but I reckon a man can't hardly do such a thing to a married woman. Well; you go on back to your bakin', or whatever you were doing." He dropped his hand and turned towards his horse. She stood small and very erect, gazing over at him.

" Paw . . .?" she murmured in a half whisper.

He swung up, settled across leather and evened up his reins. Without even looking down at her again he growled, " Oh, all right; we'll look after him too." Then he sniffed loudly and hauled his horse around looking darkly at Jim Conner. ".Well; do we sit here all the rest o' the morning, or do we get on about our business?"

Frank and John were already astride. Over across the yard Menard's men, under Lem Pierce, were moving to also mount up. Sheriff Conner dropped a slow wink to Elizabeth nodded gravely at Al Menard, who half-smiled back, then reined on around to lead the way out of the yard.

It wasn't noon yet. They had covered a lot of ground since leaving town, and not only physical ' ground ' either. Jim felt satisfied. As he headed across Menard's range away from the ranch in the general direction of Big Y's home place, he was already thinking past the arrest of Cody Younger to the trial, and how he'd work things to gain a conviction. It didn't cross his mind that he might have more than a minimum of unpleasantness over at the Younger ranch. He had the warrant and he also had three tough men riding with him. Finally, he had never sized Cody Younger up as a particularly violent man; sly and clever and unscrupulous, yes, but openly and savagely violent, no.

The Parkers were grumbling among themselves behind him. He even smiled about that, because there was no question about it; Betty had won.

CHAPTER ELEVEN

THEY SIMPLY crossed off Menard's range and onto Cody Younger's land simply by riding around a little cairn of whitewashed stones some surveyor had placed there to mark a section corner many years before.

Sheriff Conner gave a large, all-encompassing gesture with one arm. " Younger's land," he said.

The Parkers looked, were impressed, and Jeb said in a tough tone, " Yeah; some folks spend a whole lifetime buildin' up to this through damned hard work. Not Cody Younger. When a feller can forge signatures that good . . ." Jeb kept on, his words dropping sourly into the pleasant, golden day, but Sheriff Conner didn't hear them. A hard thought had just struck him. He rode for nearly a mile, then reined up out where the land was buckling and breaking up, showing rocks breaking through, like grey and weathered bones pushed out of a mummified hide. He waited until Jeb, Frank and John came abreast then he asked, fixing Jeb Parker with a steady stare, whether the Parkers had known the Overtons, up in Wyoming country.

" Sure we knew 'em," replied Jeb. " How else do you think we met Cody Younger. Carl's paw—his name was also Carl—was one of the most upstandin' men you'd ever hope to meet. Wouldn't have told a lie to save his life."

" Was he one of those folks you had in mind a while back when you said some people spend a lifetime buildin' up a good ranch?"

" He was, Sheriff. He most surely was. And Carl Overton was a man to cherish if he was your neighbour or friend. Not like young Carl, who's turned out to have Younger-blood in him, bein' a horsethief and all."

" Whoa up, Jeb. Young Carl came here to try and get something back he felt was his. He didn't steal those horses from anyone but his uncle. He by-passed a dozen big outfits to get to Big Y, and he had to ride past a dozen remudas of mighty good horseflesh. His stealin' those horses wasn't just a matter of horsestealin', and that's why I stopped here. I want you to tell me just how big this ranch was Cody Younger got away from the kid."

" Big," said old Jeb. " Sixteen good sections. Plenty of grade-cows and pure-bred bulls too. The Overton place was one of the best in the country, where we come from, Sheriff."

" Do you happen to know who Younger sold it to or how much money he got for it?"

" 'Know the feller who bought it," replied Jeb, " but don't have a very close idea of what it took to buy it." Old Jeb swung his head with an experienced eye gazing over the Big Y range which lay in all directions around them. " If all this belongs to Cody, though, I'd say he swapped dollars, Sheriff; whatever he got for the Overton place he sure ploughed back into this outfit."

" Well, that's just it, Jeb," said Sheriff Conner. " It isn't his! Big Y belongs to Carl." As the three Parkers gazed at him, Jim Conner leaned upon his saddlehorn. " Listen a minute; Cody Younger is one of the neatest forgers in the country, if I've got him figured right."

"You got him figured *exactly* right," muttered Jeb dourly.

" And I'll bet you a month's pay," went on Jim, " that if anyone cared to really make a study of it, they'd find forgery somewhere along the line in the way Cody Younger beat young Carl out of everything he owned, and took it all for himself, so he could sell out up north and come down here, buy this big ranch, and set himself up as a real cattle baron."

Jeb and Frank and John looked at Sheriff Conner for a long, quiet moment, then young John softly nodded. " Odd thing," he said in that level, quiet voice of his, " how folks can't see beyond their own damned noses when they think only of their own troubles, isn't it?"

No one answered John.

Sheriff Conner led off again, thoughtful and resolute. When they were still several miles from the Big Y home place old Jeb, who'd evidently been doing some thinking of his own, said, " Well, why didn't the boy tell someone? He didn't even talk to me about it, an' I felt sorry for the way his uncle booted him out and hired him on to work for me."

Jim thought he had the answer. " Pride works for different men different ways. I'm not saying what the kid did was right at all. In my book there's no way to justify horse stealin'. But I think I understand how the kid felt: Younger had beat him by bein' crooked, so the kid set out to do the same thing right back again."

" Hell," scorned Frank, " Carl never could've done it

like that. He's not crooked at heart, and it'd take a real crook to get ahead of Cody Younger."

Jim looked at the eldest son. " Glad you got the boy sized up that way," he said. " I felt about the same the night he broke jail and I fetched him back. He's just not good at the kind of thinkin' it takes to be an outlaw. Not even for as simple a chore as breakin' jail."

They were coming down towards some jagged red-rock spires which had once stood toweringly into the air, but which in centuries past had been tumbled to the ground, leaving only stumps standing, and a heap of red boulders, jagged and huge, lying at their base. Sheriff Conner knew this spot; around those red-rock stumps, which were perhaps ten feet taller than a mounted man, there lay a little acre-wide patch of velvet green with a spring right in the centre of it. He headed for that spot to quench his own thirst and to offer his horse a drink.

Leading them in from the north so as to avoid the biggest tumble of rocks which lay southerly and westerly, he made straight for the spring. The Parkers didn't question his lead. When they saw the water they climbed down with sighs of pleasure. It had thus far been a long morning and the day was turning off hot. First, the men tanked up, then they led up their horses, slipped the bridles off and were concentrating on this with such attention none of them heard a thing or sighted movement until three armed men rose up out of the rocks, stepped across into plain sight and levelled guns at them.

" Stand steady," a cowboy growled.

Sheriff Conner's head whipped sideways. He was looking straight into the cold, black eyes of that wiry 'breed cowboy who'd roped him off his horse, only this time the boot was on the other foot.

The three Parkers also turned their heads but otherwise didn't move at all. Cody's 'breed cowboy said something low from the corner of his mouth to the other men with guns. They at once edged around to the left and right, coming forward in such a way as to not get between the 'breed and his captives. Their purpose was clear enough; they disarmed the Parkers then also flung aside Sheriff Conner's holstered sixgun. After that the two silent rangemen backed off, keeping their prisoners covered.

Conner looked the 'breed in the eye and said, " Cowboy; you sure better know what you're doing."

Jim got his answer right back. " I know, Sheriff; I knew the other night too, only you foxed me that time." He looked the Parkers over coldly, then said, " You fellers are sure travellin' in bad company."

Jeb's voice answered, softly and quietly, " Mister; if you're figurin' on pullin' that trigger, you'd better do it and get it over with."

The 'breed eyed old Jeb closely, and lowered his sixgun. " Who are you three?" he asked. " What're you doin' on Big Y range with Conner?"

" Came by to pay a little call on your boss," said Jeb. " Whatever his name is."

" Cody Younger," growled the 'breed. " His name's Cody Younger, an' as far as you three are concerned, he don't want to see you."

" Well now, cowboy, we'll just let him tell us that himself," growled Jeb, reddening.

The 'breed's gun raised a notch and zeroed-in on Jeb's belt-buckle. " You're wrong, feller. Wrong as hell. *I'm* tellin' you, Mister Younger don't have to tell you. He told *me* and that's enough."

He flicked his pistol barrel at their horses. " You can get

astride right now, or you can stay here—permanent. I don't give a damn which."

Sheriff Conner, eyeing the 'breed, caught no inference of indecision. He eased off a little, wondering about all this. He'd never had this kind of trouble before with Big Y. It struck him as being ridiculous, too, so he said, " Put up that damned gun. We're disarmed; what more do you want?"

" Well what I want," snarled the 'breed, his eyes flashing black hatred at Jim Conner, " is to blow half your brains out for what you did to me before. So if you'll keep on talkin' tough I'll have all the excuse I need."

" To an unarmed man?" asked young John Parker.

" Keep out of it," snapped the 'breed. " The Sheriff and I've got a little private grudge between us."

" Hey," one of the other Big Y riders called across to the 'breed. " Couple riders comin' from the south."

The 'breed didn't turn but he backed up a little, got next to one of the broken red-rock spires, and stepped swiftly around it leaving Jim and the Parkers under the guns of the other two. He obviously was taking a quick look out where these other horsemen were approaching.

Sheriff Conner turned to the nearest of the other two. He'd seen the man in Lincoln a few times but didn't know him. That didn't stop him from saying the man was letting himself in for a lot of trouble, holding a gun on the legally elected law officer of the county. The cowboy's answer was a sulky shrug. The other cowboy didn't look too concerned either, so Jim gave it up and turned to the Parkers.

" Trespassing, I reckon," he murmured. " Can't be anything else."

The 'breed stepped back into sight with his cocked sixgun pointed. " We'll damned soon see what else it could be," he told Sheriff Conner. " That's Mister Younger and Wally comin'."

Conner still wasn't too worried. Then he asked a question that changed his indignation into real worry. " How come you to be down there hiding in the rocks when we rode up?" he asked.

" Simple enough," said the 'breed gruffly. " We was waitin' for you, Sheriff. We scouted you for an hour before you come over here. Then we figured you'd head for the spring, and got set."

Jim's brows curved upwards a little. This didn't make much sense unless it was a deliberate ambush. Except for besting the 'breed and having his talk with Cody Younger at the horse-corrals, he'd had no contact to speak of with either of those men. Yet what the 'breed was now implying was that he and his two companions had carefully and deliberately tried to ambush Jim and the Parkers.

" All right," said Conner. " You sprung your trap. Now tell me—why?"

The 'breed jerked his head to indicate the pair of approaching riders. He gave a cold grin. " You'll find out why," he said in a tone of stark menace.

Nothing more was said until the riders slowed to a steady walk and rode right on up behind the 'breed. Jim Conner was looking Cody Younger and Wally Walsh in the face, but only Wally was coldly looking back; Younger, his hat tipped down to protect his eyes from the sun was looking straight past Jim Conner at Jeb Parker. All three of the Parkers were glaring straight back. Younger let his breath out between closed teeth, dismounted and stepped up to the head of his horse. Finally, he shifted attention and frostily studied the lawman.

" Well, Sheriff," he murmured, " you're smarter than I

gave you credit for being. Now tell me you just happened onto these three fellers, and never saw them before this morning."

Jim looked his scorn at Cody Younger. The implication by Younger that he'd try to weasel out of this damning meeting nettled him. "When the day comes," he said coldly, "that I have to lie to scum like you, Younger, there'll be icicles in hell."

Cody nodded and let his coarse lips droop. "So you know the Parkers," he said. "And they know you. Well; that makes it easier still." Younger smiled. "In case you're wondering how this happened today, Sheriff, I'll tell you.

"Last night I just happened to be coming into town when these three men were leaving your jailhouse. I recognised them, of course, from up in western Wyoming, so I also figured out what they'd told you before leaving your office. I turned right around, rode home, and this morning had some of my men pick you four up in their sights as you left town, and trail you. My orders were to nail you good the minute you trespassed on Big Y land."

"I'm not trespassing," said Jim. "I've got a warrant for your arrest, Younger."

"Of course you have, Sheriff. For embezzlement, for forgery, for cattle stealing." Cody's smile broadened. He looked at his black-eyed 'breed and at his other armed cowboys keeping the captives under their cocked guns. "And you know something else, Sheriff? Not one damned bit of what you've learned about me is goin' to do you any good at all."

"Why not?"

Younger's smile grew thin and cruel. "Because, even without these damned Parkers from Wyoming to tell you what they know of my past, I'd still have had to kill you

D

sooner or later. I figured that out the other night, when we talked. You were getting nosy, Sheriff, and one thing I never could abide in folks, was damned nosiness— especially when it concerned me an' my affairs."

" I reckon you wouldn't like it," growled Jim Conner. " You know, Younger, I used to think that in the order of felons a murderer was worst and a horsethief came second. I've got to revise that now. What you are and what you stand for ranks right up there with a murderer."

Younger showed no anger. He flicked a close look at his four prisoners as though making certain they'd been fully disarmed, then he called the 'breed to him, sent him after his horse and the mounts of his two companions, and ordered rangeboss Wally Walsh to mount up the prisoners.

" We'll take 'em up into the broken country," he told Wally. " No one'll ever stumble across the carcasses up there."

Jim turned and slowly met the dry, glittering eyes of Jeb Parker. He stepped close and said, " Don't do anything. We're a hell of a long way from dead yet."

CHAPTER TWELVE

WHILE THEY were being herded along by the Big Y men, Jim Conner did some tall thinking. It wouldn't take any genius at all for Al Menard and Bert Neilon to read the sign left behind by he and the Parkers, and if, as Al had

intimated, he meant to make a sashay over to Big Y with
Bert and Bert's crew, to make certain Conner had encountered no difficulties, then it was entirely possible that
he and the Parkers might still come out of this alive.

There was just as good a chance they wouldn't come out
of it alive too. As far as Jim Conner's own hide was concerned, he might have survived even this meeting with his
antagonists, if only he hadn't had the Parkers along. But
Cody recognised them before he'd even opened his mouth
back there at the spring, and he figured the rest of it out
very smoothly and easily.

Jim looked at the Parkers. They were calmly riding
along, each of them thoughtfully grave and watchful. Behind the four of them were Walsh and Younger, the 'breed,
and those other two riders, all armed, all careful. From
time to time Wally and Younger would converse together
or with the 'breed. It was rather obvious to Jim Conner
that the 'breed had been in charge of the men who'd
dogged Conner's footsteps all the way from town.

That brought a sudden, chilling thought. If the 'breed
and those other two rangeriders had spied on Jim and the
Parkers all the way from town, then they'd definitely seen
Conner lead his three companions to Al Menard's ranch.
Since Al and Lem, with their cowboys, had pulled out almost immediately after Conner and the Parkers had also
left Menard's place, then perhaps the 'breed had seen that.
Moreover, if the 'breed were really observant, he'd have
seen the girl rush across Menard's yard. If he mentioned
her now, Cody Younger who'd know the Parkers up in
Wyoming, would instantly understand who she was, if he
didn't already know. From there, for a man of Younger's
temperament, it would only be a single thought before he
sent someone, perhaps the 'breed, back to get the girl too.

Without Al and his men on the ranch, she'd have less chance than a kitten.

This was of course all supposition on Jim Conner's part, but it worried him until he almost forgot where they were going and concentrated instead of making certain all of Younger's men remained in the group.

Once, Cody saw Jim turn to scan the faces. He called over to him. " Sheriff; forget it. Without a gun and out-numbered you'd never make it." Clearly, Younger was thinking Jim Conner wished to make a break for it.

The land turned subtly less hospitable and more rocky, with gnarled trees scattered across its broken, up-ended surface. They had to constantly deviate left and right to avoid erosion breaks and huge rocks half submerged in the flinty soil. This was spring range; the grass here, because of hardpan lying no more than six inches beneath the earth's surface, grew to a scant height, matured fast, and dried up within ninety days. Cowmen used this marginal land first, otherwise they'd get no benefit from it at all, but once the short-grass began to brown and wither, they drove cattle down where feed was taller and stronger.

It was possible, here and there, to dimly discern tipi-rings, indentations in the ancient earth where Indians, in generations gone, had made their camps. It was also pos-sible, if a man looked as he passed along, to see the white bones and short, heavy horns, of bison.

This part of Nebraska, though, was considered worth-less by most, and it was therefore unpopulated, and, after the spring graze was gone, it was also utterly lonely. Cattle did not drift back and there was no reason for horsemen to come here. It was, in short, as Cody Younger had sug-gested back at the spring, an ideal place to leave four corpses; no one would even come looking until the following spring, and with only a small amount of caution, he could leave Conner and the three Parkers in one of the numberless arroyos, brush-choked and unexplored, where no one would ever find them at all.

Jim Conner had no illusions about any of this. He too knew this country, so when Younger rode up beside him and motioned for Jeb and his sons to ride up ahead, the sheriff said, "You've got everything going your way, Younger, even what you've got in mind now, but there's one thing you're overlooking. We're not the only ones who know who you are and what you are."

Younger nodded. "You mean the damned kid. Conner; why didn't you just hang him like you were supposed to do? That would've made it simple all around. If you'd done that I'd have figured he hadn't told you anything about me and you'd still be alive tomorrow."

"The odd thing, Younger, is that the kid didn't want to tell me anything. He even resisted telling me his name."

"I know. That's his way. His folks were like that. I reckon they pounded it into him: If you can't speak good about someone don't speak about them at all." Younger smiled and gave his handsome head a short wag. "Funny how damned gullible folks get."

"Real funny," murmured Jim Conner dryly. "Only I wasn't just thinking of your nephew. He's not the only one who knows."

Younger's smile winked out as he sat his saddle studying Sheriff Conner. "Who else?" he asked. "Come on, Conner. I'll get it out of you one way or another." Younger jerked a thumb back where the 'breed was riding along glaring his black-eyed hatred at Jim Conner's back. "You volunteer the information or I've got a man back there who knows a hundred ways to sweat it out of you."

Conner shrugged. " It's not just one person, Younger. If that's all it was you'd only have to send one of your hired killers back into town tonight or tomorrow night to shoot someone in the back."

Cody Younger slouched along for a short way in deep thought, then he said, " I think you're lyin', Conner. You're a tight-mouthed one too. But even if you aren't, where's the proof I'm anything but what they think I am back in Lincoln?"

" That bill-of-sale you gave the Indian when you traded him Neilon's cattle for his gold."

This set Younger to speculating in silence again. Jim had hit Younger where he was sensitive and it was obvious. Younger's eyes turned grave and wondering. But Jim didn't let him come to any conclusion; he instead went right on talking, pulling his captor's attention back around.

" What in the hell were you thinking of when you did that? For gosh sakes a ten-year-old kid would've had better sense than to trade local cattle with their brands on."

" Neilon was out of the country," said Cody Younger in quick self-defence. He evidently didn't mind being accused of being a cow thief nearly as much as he minded being called stupid. " I knew he was gone, an' I also knew the redskins would be heading back up north within a day or two after I traded them the cattle, because that was part of the trade." Younger's eyes narrowed. " Then some nosy yokel had to get you into it. Even so, the bill-of-sale prevented you from doing anything until Neilon returned, and right after you left the redskin camp I went over to tell them to get under way and to keep moving until they were out of Nebraska. They did, too, so even when Neilon got back there wasn't a damned thing anyone could do."

Jim shook his head in mild wonderment. " All that for

five hundred bucks worth of Wyoming gold? Younger; it wasn't worth it, unless you've got a hell of a weakness for raw gold."

"It's a hobby of mine," explained Younger. "Everything else loses value, but not gold. I've been collecting the stuff for years. Someday I'll find a man with enough of it and sell this ranch for more gold. 'Anything wrong with that, Conner?"

Jim had seen gold-fever in men before. Even in honest men it worked a subtle change turning them avaricious, mean, juiceless and grasping. "I reckon not," he quietly averred. "An old feller I knew years back who also had the fever told me his gold hoard took the place of wife and family. That it was more loyal than a man's best friends. That his way of life could come to an end the very next day, and whatever came afterwards would still use raw gold to base reconstruction upon."

"Your old friend," stated Cody Younger, "was a very clever man."

"Yeah," replied Jim Conner, very dryly. "He overlooked one thing: Gold may be more loyal than friends, but in this case it also drew more enemies. We found him one morning with his throat cut from ear to ear and his hoard of gold gone."

Cody Younger made a long study of Conner's profile before he said, "It's too bad you an' I are on opposite sides, Conner. I keep thinkin' we'd have been a hard combination to beat if we'd been pardners."

"I'm not a good forger, Younger, and even less good as a thief."

Cody smiled with his lips but not his eyes. "It was just a thought, Conner. Just a thought."

After that they rode along until Wally Walsh called for

specific directions. Then Cody reined off and dropped back to ride with his rangeboss and the three lethal-faced cowboys. They were by then into even wilder, more broken and rocky country.

Something occurred which inspired Younger to detach one of his men and send him down their back-trail. The Parkers noticed this and so did Jim Conner. For the sheriff at least, who understood that any of the darkly twisted arroyos they were now skirting around could be the one Younger had in mind dumping their bodies into, even this slight diversion was welcome.

Jim couldn't see anything back there, though; no riders, no dust scuffed to life under horses' hooves, not even any reason for Younger to be anxious now that they were all deep into his northernmost, wildly jumbled and darkly timbered uplands range.

Jeb Parker let his two sons drop back and ride with Jim Conner.

Younger didn't object and although the black-eyed venomous 'breed glared, he said nothing. Old Jeb said quietly and too casually, " Mighty rough country up in here, Mister Conner. A bunch of bodies, if they was hid right, wouldn't even attract buzzards, would they?" Jim didn't answer; he didn't get a chance to answer because Jeb went right on in the same casual, quiet, monotonous tone of voice, pushing out words whose meaning was as obvious as the dazzling overhead sunlight.

Jim stopped looking rearward and concentrated on Parker. The older man was clearly up to something. Jeb turned, caught Jim's attention, and reached down to scratch his stomach. While doing this Jeb kept right on making that unimportant conversation. His scratching fingers pulled open his shirt-front and Sheriff Conner's puzzled eyes caught sight of the small, black-rubber, curved, parrot's-beak grip of a .41 calibre under-and-over derringer pistol. A hide-out gun; the kind card-sharks, professional gunfighters, and sometimes honest men also carried, when they had reason to believe they might be in hostile country.

Jeb stopped scratching and mightily yawned, spat aside and turned to lay a sardonic, wry expression upon Conner. He was finished talking evidently for now he poked along until Younger called a halt, looking dispirited or demoralised, or sleepy, and for the life of Jim Conner he couldn't decide which it was.

They halted to wait for that cowboy Younger had previously sent back, to catch on up to them. He was coming, but he looked ant-size back down there crossing out of the good range into the badlands.

Younger's 'breed never took his eyes off Jim Conner unless Cody Younger spoke to him, and that wasn't very often. He obviously had murder in his mind as well as in his heart.

" Smoke if you like," said Younger to his prisoners. He was indifferent about it and fished inside his coat for a cigar which he lazily lighted and puffed upon.

John Parker didn't smoke. His brother Frank as well as his father did though, and so did Sheriff Conner. They made cigarettes and deeply inhaled, exhaled and kept their wary glances running back and forth, up and down. The Parker boys, Jim understood, knew about their father's hide-out pistol. Jim's hopes weakly soared when he speculated that perhaps all three of the Parkers had derringers. If that were so, then their position was a long way from hopeless.

Jeb looked straight at Jim, his narrowed eyes quizzical,

and minutely shook his head as though he'd just read Conner's thoughts. The 'breed growled at Jeb. " Hey, old man; you tryin' to tell Conner somethin'?"

Parker turned and ran a scornful glance up and down the 'breed, turned his head with monumental disdain and spat. The cowboy's jaw muscles humped up into a straining ridge of pure gristle. His black eyes got very still. He was a half-breed; from earliest childhood he had been held in contempt by both races, red one and white one. But he was a man now and an armed one. He called Jeb a fighting name in a voice so low it was almost a whisper, dropping his gun-hand straight down. Cody Younger evidently recognised the signs, for he turned and called sharply.

" That's enough! You'll get your chance, dammit. If you keep baitin' 'em you're goin' to get it right back. Leave 'em alone until I give you the word—then you carve your initials on their naked bellies for all I care."

The 'breed's wrath didn't subside but he didn't draw the gun, and that was what had Jim Conner holding his breath.

Eventually the back-tracking scout caught up and rode the last hundred or two feet shaking his head. " Must've been somethin' else," he reported to Younger. " I didn't see no dust back there an' no riders."

Younger kept studying the back-trail even after receiving this report. He evidently had seen something back there, or had thought he had seen something, and such was his reliance upon his own judgement that although he'd sent back a man and had been told there was nothing back there, he was still sceptical.

In the end though, he squared up in the saddle and jutted out his chin. " Lead out, Sheriff," he called. " Angle off a little to your left."

Jim obeyed, riding slowly and going over in his mind's eye all the places which lay northwesterly from their present position where a successful massacre could be undertaken. There was one place which stuck in his mind, but until he'd been instructed to swing over towards it, he'd entirely forgotten: Four caves at the base of a lightning-shattered cliff-face Indians had used for thousands of years as places to hide and to sleep safely during bad storms.

He looked around. Younger was smoking his cigar looking pleased and confident. Jim knew then he meant to kill them in the caves, fill whichever hole he preferred with stones afterwards, and what Younger was clearly thinking would be correct: Killed and buried like that, no one would ever find Jim Conner or the Parkers.

CHAPTER THIRTEEN

THEY BEGAN riding through boulder fields, and looming ahead was the low, black and beetling cliff-face of a massive upland plateau. They were approaching the base of it. Southward from that bluff a watcher would be able to command a good view down across the broken badlands, even out across part of the distant prairie in the general direction of Lincoln. It was no wonder prehistoric men chose that cliff-base; it offered shelter from the weather, protection to the rear from warring enemies, and it also

presented them with a hunter's paradise, because all they
had to do was sit in the doorway of their caves and watch
southward for animal movement.

As a grave, though, which is how Jim considered the
caves they were heading for, he thought the prehistoric
hide-out even better yet.

Cody Younger called for another halt. This time he dismounted, flung his reins to one of the cowboys and walked
back where a mighty oak stood, stepped up beside it and
leaned with his back to them all, standing like stone and
watching the back-trail.

He stood like that for a full ten minutes before turning,
strolling back and halting near the cowboy he'd previously
sent back. " Maybe you're blind as well as dumb," he said
softly, " or maybe you're treacherous." He turned and held
up a rigid arm. " Watch," he commanded, and slowly
lowered the arm.

They all watched, Sheriff Conner, Jeb and his two sons,
Younger, Walsh, the cowboys and the black-eyed 'breed. It
was the latter who finally grunted deep down, nodding his
head.

" One man," he said. " One little thin drift of dust." He
looked down at Younger. " I'll go down and wait in the
rocks. If you hear a shot you'll know I got him. All right?"

Cody twisted to gaze at his hireling. He nodded. " If you
shoot make it good," he muttered, then watched as the
'breed angled back down-country the way they'd recently
come. When the cowboy was lost to sight he turned.
" Sheriff; you sure better hope it's not some friend of
yours."

" I'll do that," grumbled Conner, straining hard to make
out the horseman, and failing. " You've got pretty good
eyesight, Younger."

They all dismounted. The heat was considerable here, rolling back down to them off the black stone of the cliff-face. There was no water so the men quietly sweated and stood patient.

Jeb Parker spoke to Younger for the first time in more than an hour. He asked where, exactly, Younger was taking them. Cody turned and pointed towards the cliff-base, turned back and didn't say a word but returned to watching that thin feather of dun dust coming straight up along their back-trail.

Jeb turned, scanned the yonder cliff and screwed up his eyes. He patently didn't understand. Conner said, " There are some prehistoric cliffs at the base. One of 'em'll be our grave."

Cody turned his head, eyeing Jim Conner. " You're dead right, Sheriff. *Dead* right."

When they could make out the oncoming rider plainly enough to distinguish man from mount, they stood stiffly waiting. The 'breed had to be down there hiding somewhere, drawing his bead, giving the horseman another hundred or two yards in order to make certain of his kill. They waited and sweated but there was no gun-shot.

Wally Walsh said, " One of our own riders, Cody." Younger spat out his dead cigar and walked over into some tree-shade nearby without comment. Jim Conner thought Younger looked worried.

Finally, the oncoming rider was joined by another horseman, who turned out to be the 'breed. The pair of them came directly up.

Younger's freshly arrived rider was sweaty, rumpled and red in the face. His horse was white-lathered and tuckered too. He singled out Cody and swung a heavy arm to indi-

cate the southerly range. " Riders quarterin' for sign down
there," he panted. " Menard with his crew an' Neilon with
his men, Mister Younger. They come to the ranch. I seen
'em an' lit out first."

Cody was cold towards this man. " And they followed
your dust up until you led them right to our tracks headin'
north," he said, reaching down to ease off the tie-down
holding his sixgun in its holster. " You damned moron if it
wasn't so noisy I'd kill you right here." Younger stepped
away from the shade and stood a long while studying the
back-country. He still had a hand lying upon the graceful
curve of his sixgun handle.

The 'breed and Wally Walsh bent to whisper in low
tones briefly, then Walsh walked on over where Younger
stood and said something Jim couldn't hear. He also
pointed off to their right where the country was almost
solid rock. Jim could imagine what this fresh suggestion en-
compassed: If they made for the tallis and flat-stone
country to the right, no one could track them.

But Jim had guessed only half of it. He discovered that
in a moment, when Younger narrowed his eyes in long
thought, then eventually gave Wally a curt nod saying,
" All right; it'll probably work at that. I'll lead off over
there. You take the prisoners and one man as soon as we're
in the rocks so's they'll be unable to see we've split up, and
head for the caves. Wait for me there. Guard 'em close and
wait for me."

They got back astride and headed to the northeast now,
riding through an increasingly stony, rough country until
they came at last to level, wind-scoured fields of nearby
stone. As Sheriff Conner viewed what lay ahead he thought
this ruse never would have fooled an Indian for shod-horses
left tracks over rock which barefoot horses wouldn't leave

at all. But—and this is what made the big difference—
those men back there with Al Menard and Bert Neilon
weren't redskins; they'd be slowed to a crawl and eventually forced to give it up altogether because there wasn't a
real tracker among them. There weren't any genuine
trackers left in the whole country for that matter. Cowboys
like the men with Menard and Neilon could make out an
obvious trail well enough, but without dust to catch im-
prints they'd be lost.

Jim watched the route they were following. It was while
he was keeping an eye upon the marks being ever so faintly
brushed over stone by the horse's feet ahead of him that the
idea came. He fished for his tobacco sack but didn't make a
smoke. He instead pouched up a big cud of tobacco and
chewed. As often as necessity dictated he also spat great
gobbets of dark brown juice. Not being a real chewer he
was very careful not to swallow any of the juice. Few
things could make a non-chewer deathly ill to his stomach
as swallowing a mouthful of tobacco juice.

The sun was working its way around towards the cliff
which lay due west of them. Shadows began to appear here
and there in the broken jumble of wild country they were
now traversing. This didn't seem to bother Cody Younger,
and in fact he probably enjoyed the possibility of nightfall
coming. In darkness he could slip away from the pursuit
very easily.

He halted them, finally, where a long trough passed east
to west, looked at the prisoners and smiled. Gesturing to the
'breed and Wally Walsh, he said, " You'll be in right good
hands, Sheriff. As soon as I'm sure your friends are lost or
discouraged, I'll come on over to the caves and we'll finish
this thing." His smile winked out. He nodded at the 'breed,
who eased up behind the prisoners and snarled. Wally

Walsh led the way down into the westerly trough in the hills.

Sheriff Conner turned to glance back just once. The 'breed gave him a vicious jab in the back with the end of his carbine. " Look ahead," he snarled. " Nothin' for you to see back there. The others are already gone. Hell; your friends couldn't find us in here after dark if they had a whole troop of cavalry an' a bushel of coal-oil lamps."

Wally Walsh finally turned southward leading the way back towards the front of the cliff-face, but he'd chosen a particularly brushy little arroyo to pass through. The men swore and their mounts flinched. Chaparral thorns nearly two inches long inflicted painful wounds. The 'breed accepted this stoically but Walsh didn't. He swore often and fiercely before they broke out into the clear again. They were by this time far enough west to be close to the cliff-face and, as Jim Conner recalled, not more than a half or perhaps three-quarters of a mile from the old caves.

" Quiet," hissed Walsh, twisting in his saddle. They all reined up and sat perfectly still. Somewhere over in the eastward stonefields men softly called back and forth. Jim recognised Al Menard's voice once, and later he also heard Bert Neilon's particularly fierce way of swearing.

The 'breed chuckled. It sounded like a rattlesnake giving his warning. " They're stumblin' all over theirselves over in there," the 'breed said. " Head out, Wally, there's nothin' to worry about."

Walsh reined off to his right, worked his way up as far as the narrow buck-run which lay along the front base of the cliff, and almost at once they all passed into a hot kind of sooty world of shadows and fetid air.

Jeb Parker was directly behind Jim Conner. Frank Parker was behind his father and young John rode just ahead of the 'breed. In this single-file procession they walked their animals straight along making scarcely any sound at all, for this little game trail they were upon had been in use since the world was young; whatever gravel had once lined it was now worn down to a powdery grey dust that smelt strongly of alkali.

Wally lifted his arm finally, pointing. "There's the first one."

It was a cave, but with a very low opening. So low in fact that white men would have to bend double to even get inside. The 'breed said to keep going; there were two larger ones about a mile ahead. Wally nodded and dropped his arm. Jim twisted to look back and Jeb carefully dropped one eyelid, then sprang it straight up again. Jeb didn't seem worried at all, now. Behind him, Frank and young John were as impassive and quiet as stone. Neither of them even flicked a glance at Sheriff Conner.

The afternoon light was at last beginning to steadily fail. Once, Walsh, riding a few yards in front, startled a bobcat from its mossy bed near a little sulphur spring. The tawny little animal was gone in a flash of grey-white movement.

They finally reached the second cave. It was a little larger than the first hole had been, but not much. They rode right by it without even hesitating. Like all these ancient holes in the cliff-face, there was an ingrained blackness part way up the overhead rock where ancient smoky fires had left their scald and black, pitchy scorch.

The third cave was a large eyeless socket, nearly round and with nothing in front of it for some little distance, except tumbled rocks and gritty soil. Here, Wally halted to bend from his saddle and look inside. He evidently hadn't ever been in any of these caves, as indeed few white men had. The 'breed called ahead. " Go on, Wally; there's one more up ahead. It's big enough to bury four men in real nice."

They resumed their way, came to the last cave, and halted. Jim Conner gazed at the black-stained big opening. Here, the land rose to a gentle rise right up to the entrance, then broke away east and west, which gave the cave an appearance of height. There were trees growing close by, but generally the ground at this place was as flinty and sterile as it had been back by the immediately preceding cave.

Walsh dismounted, flexed his legs, and jerked his head at the captives indicating they should also get down. No one spoke until the 'breed came walking up holding out his hand for their reins. " You won't need 'em any more," he said, referring to their horses. " I'll take 'em off through the trees an' tie 'em until we're through with what we got to do here."

When the 'breed reached for Sheriff Conner's reins, Jim held them out, then, just short of the 'breed's outstretched fingers, let them drop. At once the cowboy's black eyes flamed with a wild, murderous light and he reached with the speed of a striking snake. Jim had known that blow was coming; he rolled his head to avoid and brought up a fist which caught the cowboy just under the heart. It wasn't a hard punch because Conner couldn't get himself set first, but it knocked the 'breed backwards with his mouth open.

Wally Walsh's sixgun snapped into full cock in his right fist. He snarled at them both, swearing coldly. Sheriff Conner was finished; all he'd meant to do was enrage the 'breed and he'd certainly succeeded. The cowboy stood ten feet away, his dark murderous eyes fixed with an intense brightness on Conner. He seemed either ready to spring at Jim or draw his holstered sixgun. It was the harsh, icily dropping words of Walsh that held him back, but for a moment no one, perhaps not even the 'breed himself, was sure what he would do.

Jeb Parker stood back there scratching his middle and brightly watching the half-breed.

"You shoot him," said Wally, finally, " an' they'll hear the noise for three miles in all directions. Now get his lousy horse and go on."

The 'breed came up out of his coiled crouch very slowly, very stiffly. He minced forward, caught the reins and said, " Conner; it's goin' to take you two, three days to die under those rocks when I'm through with you."

Wally was getting impatient. He flicked his gun. " Get the damned horses out of here," he snarled at the 'breed. " I'll keep 'em right here until you get back. Move, damn it, I'm tired of this monkey business between you'n that lousy lawman !"

After the 'breed walked off Jeb Parker gazed upon Walsh and softly said, " Mister; we're plumb alone now. How would you like to sell Younger and that half-breed out for two thousand dollars?"

Walsh's hawk-like lean face slowly split into a death's-head grin. " Where would you get two thousand dollars, feller? Why; from the looks of you it'd tax you to the limit just to buy a forty dollar saddle. Forget it. Even if you had that kind of money it'd be almighty risky. Now just shut up and stand still, the bunch of you."

Sheriff Conner let off a long breath, turned and traded a sardonic look with the Parkers, jerked a thumb towards the big cave and said, " Pretty fancy grave at that. The whole cliff'll be our monument." He spat amber and turned back as the 'breed came padding up again.

CHAPTER FOURTEEN

SUMMER DAYLIGHT had a habit of lingering on and on, even after dusk ordinarily should have turned off into evening. But inside that stale-musty old cave it was like stepping right from daylight into midnight. The entire inside of the place was smoked over until not one speck of white granite showed anywhere. The ground underfoot was a gritty combination of pulverised stone and prehistoric bones, ground together over the centuries into a pale, acrid powder. Someone had once sat with his back to the fire-ring in the centre of the cave and laboriously scratched the figure of a gigantic bison into the living stone. Afterwards it was anyone's guess how many hundreds of generations had sat in the smoke eyeing that crude outline.

The cave wasn't more than fifteen feet deep. From some jagged overhead stone-points it was safe to assume that originally the cave hadn't been more than perhaps ten or twelve feet into the cliff. But some enterprising prehistoric man had set about deepening it. This was probably what caused the ground just beyond the front opening to be higher than all the ground surrounding it.

The stone-ring in the centre of the cave was so seared and tempered that striking any of the boulders together resulted in their immediately crumbling to dust. The 'breed did that, struck two of the rocks together, then dropped them at his feet rolling his eyes over at the bison etched upon the wall. He also walked to the back of the cave and thumped the wall.

Wally wasn't interested in anything but the prisoners. He obviously didn't like being in these confining quarters with them and growled for them to sit down on the ground and keep their hands where he could see them.

When the 'breed sauntered back he stopped in front of Sheriff Conner, stooped, picked up a handful of the ancient, rank dust, and flicked into Jim's face. He was springing backwards with the agility of a cat even as he did this, so when Jim closed his eyes against the dust and lashed out at the same time, he only struck air. The 'breed laughed. The sound made a peculiar, vibrating kind of echo in the cave.

Wally glared. " Cut that out you damned fool," he snarled, his back to the wall, his right hand lying lightly upon his holstered sixgun. Wally clearly did not like either the interior of the cave, nor the close proximity of his prisoners.

But the 'breed seemed just the opposite. While he'd been jumpy and quick to snarl on the trail, after he was inside the cave with the captives he seemed to loosen and reflect a feeling of security.

Jeb sat sphinx-like with one of his sons on each side, scratching his middle and eyeing Wally Walsh's dangling sixgun. The range was perfect for Jeb's little snub-nosed forty-one calibre, but he needed better than a fifty-fifty break with Wally to succeed. Right from the start of their captivity, even though their captors were at times almost scornfully indifferent to them as sources of danger, they were never quite off-guard; some one of them invariably was watching with a gun in hand, as now, or there were too many of them for that little belly-gun which only held two bullets in its two barrels.

The 'breed dropped to his hunkers, eased out his sixgun and raised it to idly spin the cylinder and maliciously sight down its short barrel straight at Sheriff Conner. The 'breed grinned. Quite obviously, right up until the time they'd entered this cave, he'd been about equal parts apprehensive and uncertain. Now, all that was changed. He grinned often—cruelly, to be sure—but he grinned none the less, and he handled himself with more solid assurance.

"Like a lousy tarantula," said Jim Conner to him. "Brave as all hell with a rock wall at your back, 'breed, but out in daylight a hell of a lot less than a real man."

The 'breed didn't answer that at all. He just squatted across the rank stone room, eyes blackly glittering, showing the prisoners his white-toothed, bleak and menacing smile.

"Get it out of your system," he told Sheriff Conner. "When the boss gets back here, tin-badge, you're goin' to find out how I've been plannin' things for you." The 'breed waved a hand carelessly towards Jeb and Frank and young John. He didn't even look at them. "These others—kneel 'em down an' shoot 'em in the ear. Get it over with them. They ain't important at all. But you, Sheriff; you're somethin'; I've been figurin' ways to make you scream."

Jim Conner's flesh crawled; he wasn't afraid exactly, it was more revulsion. He turned to Wally and said, "All right if we make a smoke?"

Walsh grunted indifferently and stepped gingerly past the 'breed to go over closer to the cave's entrance for a quick look out.

Jeb and Frank gravely set about making their smokes. Because Jim Conner had given his tobacco away back at the jailhouse he had to wait his turn. Jeb held off lighting up until he could save one match by lighting up for himself and Sheriff Conner. He couldn't say anything, their captors were much too close to miss even a whisper, but Jeb could use his eyes to convey a quiet message of assurance, and he did.

The 'breed was holding his sixgun dangling between his knees, black eyes watching with a ferret-like intensity. Wally remained by the opening beyond which daylight lingered stubbornly even though shadows were lying along the far side of trees and rocks out there.

" Mister," drawled rawboned, stringy Frank Parker, addressing the 'breed. " I'm kind of curious about something : Did you fellers who work for Cody Younger hire on down here in Nebraska ?"

The cowboy gazed at Frank as though trying to guess the speculation behind that question. Then he said, " Yeah; but it was Wally here who done the recruitin'. He sort of rode aroun' lookin' for a special kind o' rangerider. Ain't that right, Wally ?"

Walsh turned and nodded, then turned back to studying the yonder daylight without saying a word. Wally was more than ever anxious to get this over with.

Frank seemed momentarily satisfied. But moments later he again addressed the 'breed cowboy. " Then I reckon none of you knew Cody in Wyoming. Would you like me to tell you how he's looked on up there ?"

" It don't matter," growled Wally, spearing Frank with a hostile scowl. " An' if you're leadin' up to another try at a bribe, feller, forget it."

The 'breed, who hadn't been on hand when old Jeb had made that other offer, pricked up his ears. " What bribe ?" he asked, shooting Walsh a quick, interested look.

Wally answered while still gazing anxiously out of their

cave. " That older one tried to get me to sell out. While you was takin' care of the horses he offered me two thousand dollars to let 'em go."

The 'breed's gaze swiftly jumped over to Jeb. " Two thousand . . ." He leaned a little from the waist. " Hey feller," he said in a voice suddenly dripping with tight avarice. " Empty out your pockets."

" Ah hell," growled Wally, turning. " You don't believe they'd have that kind of cash do you?"

The 'breed was so absorbed in his sudden anticipation he missed Walsh's scoffing tone. " I said empty out your damned pockets," he repeated, lifting his sixgun towards Jeb.

For several bad moments no one spoke nor moved. Eventually Jeb said, " Cowboy; if I empty my pockets you're not goin' to find anything."

" No?"

" No!"

" Then where, you old devil?"

" Half of it's in one boot, half of it's in the other boot."

There was something in Jeb's voice that rang of truth. Wally Walsh slowly straightened up over against the cave's opening and turned to watch. His sixgun was holstered. He made no move to touch it. Jim Conner, who was watching Walsh from between narrowed lids, thought Wally was just beginning to wonder if after all he hadn't been mistaken.

" All right then," murmured the 'breed, leaning still more and forgetting, evidently, that he was holding his dangling sixgun between his knees as he hunkered over against the granite west wall. " Haul off your boots."

" All right," agreed Jeb, but making no move to obey as he stared straight into the 'breed's face. " Only first off we're goin' to palaver a little. I'll give you the two thousand. You walk out of here with us and turn your backs while we get away."

The 'breed's reply was perfunctory. " You darned old idiot; *we* got the guns. You don't make no terms. I can shoot you an' afterwards take your boots off."

" Like hell you can. One gunshot inside this lousy cave'll sound like a cannon outside. Those possemen'll hear it sure. By now they might even be workin' their way back towards this hole anyway."

The 'breed thought a moment, then softly smiled. Without any vestige of argument, he nodded. " Show us the money, and we'll just maybe set you loose at that."

Jim Conner's lips drooped with scorn. If that 'breed thought his prisoners were that naïve he was childish. He had no intention of setting anyone loose.

But Jeb seemed satisfied. He raised one lanky leg and grunted at tugging off his left boot. No one moved or made a sound. They were all watching with an absorbed, hard interest. The boot came off.

Jeb grinned at the look on Wally's face; it showed an I-told-you-so expression of disgusted triumph. The other guard didn't abandon his avarice that easily. " Up-end it," he snarled. Jeb obeyed and a flat, damp little thin pad of greenbacks dropped out. Sheriff Conner, watching Walsh, would have laughed under other circumstances. Wally's hawkish features dissolved with a look of purest astonishment. He and the 'breed squatted less than fifteen feet away staring round-eyed at the bills of large denomination.

Walsh said, " I'll be damned," in a hushed, awed tone of voice.

The 'breed recovered first. " Yank off the other boot," he ordered.

Jeb carefully lay his left boot in his lap, raised his right

foot slowly and, using only his left hand on the heel, began
to rock his foot back and forth to loosen the leather. He did
this with considerable slow effort, still wearing his little
tough grin and keeping his eyes upon the 'breed, who, like
Lionel Walsh, was intently straining towards the loosening
right boot. Once, Jeb flicked a stabbing look at Sheriff
Conner and signalled with an infinitesimal nod. Jim
tightened up into coiled readiness. Jeb was concentrating
on the 'breed, who still had that sixgun dangling between
his knees, but his grip on the thing was now loose and unconcerned; he was leaning forward watching the boot and
Jeb Parker's left hand which was working the boot loose.

Walsh's sixgun was still holstered. He had both hands out
front. When Conner moved he had to catapult himself
across the cave straight at Walsh; had to reach him head-on
before the rangeboss could rock back and dive for his gun.

"Damned thing sure fits tight on m'right foot," muttered Jeb. "Strange how every pair o' boots a man owns
always fits tight on one foot or the other."

"Well dammit all *pull*," panted the 'breed.

Jeb drew his right leg up higher across his lap. He gave a
grunt and a harder tug. The boot slipped off his heel and
began to slide down. Jeb's right hand was underneath the
left boot, which lay in his lap. Then he gave a final tug and
the right boot came completely off. He held it up, Wally's
and the 'breed's eyes intently following it. Very slowly, grinning broadly but with a deadly glitter in his eyes, Jeb
Parker up-ended the boot. Another flat pad of large-
denomination bills fell to the cave's dusty floor.

That was when Jeb fired. The explosion was tremendous
inside the cave. But it also acted as the releasing mechanism
for Jim Conner, who only caught one blurry view of the
'breed's head slamming violently backwards as Jeb's bullet

hit him plumb centre, its impact at this deadly range, being like the hammer-blow strike of a powerful fist. That was all Jim had time to see before his right shoulder drove straight into Wally Walsh's chest knocking the rangeboss back against the unrelenting stone too.

Walsh exploded into a snarling, kicking-out, lashing pinwheel of arms and legs. He didn't have time to go for his gun. He only had time to whip sideways before that hurtling body hit him. But he did manage, even in the split second he had, to realise what had happened, to suck around enough so that he missed the full, pulverising effect of Conner's lunge.

Then he tried to grab his sixgun, but then it was too late.

Jim wasn't concentrating so much on hitting Walsh as he was on getting hold of Wally's right arm at the wrist. He got it in both hands and clung with desperate stubbornness. Wally tried heaving himself backwards, towards the opening of the cave. Conner's solid weight stopped him like a dog being fetched up short on the end of a chain. Walsh raised his left and beat Conner around the head and shoulders. He didn't have the power in his left, though, which he probably had in his right. Still, the strikes hurt and Conner pushed his face against Walsh's rank shirt-front to save his eyes. Then, finding he could control Walsh's gun-hand with only one of his hands, he eased off with his right, twisted backwards and hammered a vicious strike into Walsh's soft parts. The rangeboss's teeth rattled as a great whoosh of breath burst out.

Conner felt the body under him turning soggy. He reared back a second time and struck again, putting all the force he could manage into the blow. That time Walsh's face contorted as the last of his wind was slammed out. He opened his mouth wide to scream and no sound came. His eyes rolled aimlessly. His gun-arm went limp. Conner eased back looking at the grey lips and dimming eyes. With Walsh's resistance gone, he yanked away the rangeboss's sixgun, rocked back onto his heels and shot straight up. Walsh turned, writhing on the floor in agony and feebly clawing at his battered middle.

Frank and John were standing above him too, now, but it was all over. Walsh finally passed out and lay face down in the ancient dust.

Jim turned. The 'breed was sitting slumped against the cave wall, horribly grinning and dead from Jeb's bullet. Underfoot lay the trampled green bills which had brought death to one of Cody Younger's killers, and unconsciousness to another one.

CHAPTER FIFTEEN

JEB SLOWLY put his derringer back inside his waistband and slowly turned away from his victim. Frank scooped up the 'breed's sixgun. Sheriff Conner had Walsh's pistol. The only unarmed one was young John who glided past and looked out, stepped through into the heavy, silent atmosphere and looked all around before jerking his head. As the others also stepped out Jim Conner thought he detected a sound far off of steel striking stone.

" Find the horses," he said swiftly, turning to run. Jeb called sharply and pointed into the cave. He asked about

Walsh. Sheriff Conner said, " To hell with him. Let's get away from here !"

The 'breed hadn't taken their horses very far. They located the bosque of trees where he'd tied them by the stamping sounds.

While the others retrieved their own mounts Conner went to the pair of Big Y horses, hung their bridles over each saddlehorn, turned the horses and slapped each of them across the rump setting them free. Wally and the 'breed cowboy weren't going to need them any more; at least the 'breed surely wasn't going to.

They left the area of their cave strung out, the Parkers following Jim Conner, who led them straight along the cliff-face westerly as far as the first brush-choked gloomy canyon which was a kind of cul-de-sac raising almost straight up at its rear reaches where not even a goat could have climbed out.

John pointed out the risk of them all being caught in this place. Sheriff Conner replied that he was aware, but that he'd thought he'd detected riders coming back down by the cave and wanted primarily to get out of sight until he could scout along on foot down there to make certain, after which they'd try to get completely away, locate Al Menard and Bert Neilon with their riders, then come back for Younger.

He handed John his reins and pausing just long enough to inspect the sixgun he'd taken from Walsh, stepped back out of the protective canyon to start southward out and around, through the yonder trees and boulders.

As though from a great distance someone's voice came through on a little meandering wind. Conner stopped beside an old broken-crowned oak tree trying to guess where that man had called from, but the call was not repeated so all he could deduce was that someone actually was approaching. It was too dangerous, waiting around to ascertain whether this might be friends or foes. Moreover, since the call had been faint even though the man who'd made it must have yelled as loudly as he could, it also meant whoever was coming was still a long way off.

Jim hastened back, grabbed his reins, got astride and with only a peremptory gesture with one arm, saying nothing at all, led the Parkers out of the gloomy cul-de-sac, turning westerly once more and hastening along the front of the rough old forbidding cliff-face.

They passed along to the west until Jeb said in a pleasant tone of voice he thought they'd out-distanced whoever was back there. That might have been a signal for exactly the opposite to be true, for a rifle cracked, a lead bullet struck stone on Frank Parker's right, splintered rock and sent deadly slivers in all directions.

With a loud grunt of astonishment Frank ducked and twisted rearwards in his saddle. The younger brother, farther back, had evidently been the target, for when Sheriff Conner stared down there, a puff of oily smoke was rising from a clump of trees they'd recently passed, and John Parker was the closest to the rifleman and farther back than any of the others.

Jim stepped off with his sixgun moving. " Go on," he called to the Parkers. " Due west, Jeb. I'll catch up. Make tracks!"

Jeb shot past calling upon his boys to follow after. Jim Conner loosened two rapid shots into that distantly rearward clump of trees, saw the brush and leaves violently quiver, and knew that whether he'd scored a hit or not he'd certainly inspired sudden movement in someone down there.

Conner took his horse southward where several enormous

rocks leaned into one another. He left the horse back out of harm's path, skirted around and came out alongside the farthest side of the smooth, grey-stone monoliths.

There was no movement back up in the trees. He searched elsewhere in all that shadowy, broken, rocky and tree-speckled countryside. There was no movement anywhere, but all that had to mean was that the rifleman, evidently a reckless scout for Younger, had gotten too far ahead, and was now lying low because he knew the gunshots would bring him reinforcements.

Conner didn't want to get pinned down at all. He went back to his horse, got astride and tried riding straight away so that the boulders were always between his back and the muzzle of someone's rifle back there. It worked for nearly a hundred yards, then another rifle-shot spat sound and lead. Conner was peering over one shoulder and saw where the rifleman had fired from this time. He had indeed moved, and instead of contenting himself lying close back there, he was still aggressively trying to get closer as swiftly as he dared.

Conner raised his sixgun to fire where the smoke-puff arose. In fact he had his trigger-finger curling against the light pull of the captured gun, when over on his right closer to the diminishing cliff-face, a sixgun opened up in an angry, raking blaze of gunfire. The hand-gun sounded almost like a company of volley-firing soldiers its owner was thumbing off his single-shot blasts so rapidly. Whichever of the Parkers that was over there, Conner thought, was no slouch with a hand-gun.

This time the hidden rifleman got enough. Jim Conner had to leave the shielding shelter of his monoliths and lope riskily straight across an open place, but the gunman back there didn't open fire again.

When he came up, Jeb and Frank were grinning. Frank had the sixgun. He was re-loading it. Young John was farther back holding their three nervous mounts. Conner called that it was good shooting, then gestured for them to get astride. He led them more swiftly now, since obviously those approaching riders back there had been the Big Y men, and also quite obviously they'd found their dead 'breed companion and their severely punished range-boss.

" Where'n hell," asked Jeb, as he loped behind Sheriff Conner, " are those friends of yours?"

Jim had no idea. All he felt certain of was that whether Neilon and Menard knew where the others were before, now, after those angry gunshots in the twilight hush, they'd be able to tell by sounds. Still, as he turned to say back to Jeb Parker, it didn't matter, exactly, where help was; what mattered was that the Parkers and Jim Conner either get away before they were shot down by men with rifles, which they did not have and could not match, or else through a very improbable divine intercession, stumbled upon a cache of rifles, they had to keep moving.

Where the cliff-face broke, finally, heaving northward in a flung-back fashion which trickled down to a low series of canyons and stony gulches, Conner was able finally to get clear. Before that he'd had to remain pinned along the cliff-face. Here too, although there was plenty of thornpin-brush, there were even greater expanses where grass and rocks and trees were the only impediments to travel.

" You know this badlands-country?" asked Jeb, sceptic-ally looking around.

Jim knew it; he'd hunted it for both men and meat. He pointed towards the shallow canyon lying dead ahead a half mile. The brush in there seemed impenetrable.

" Through that opening there's a spring and a grassy place about ten acres in size."

Jeb eyed the brush doubtingly but made no objection. They eventually got over there, ploughed profanely through, burst forth beyond the choking brush precisely as Jim Conner had said into an elysian little secret vale, and for the first time all day, relaxed every nerve and muscle.

The back of their canyon tapered off onto a higher plateau. There was a trail winding down from up there both broad and deep-cut. Deer, wild cattle, horses, mountain lions, bobcats, every conceivable kind of wildlife had used that trail since time out of mind. Jeb studied it carefully and nodded. " Good back door," he said, stepping off to take his mount across where a trickle of cold water ran from a cleft in black stone to form a marshy little pool. " Sheriff; so far you're doin' just fine."

John said mildly, " Sure enough, Sheriff, but there's one miracle I'd surely appreciate if you can arrange that too : A carbine."

Conner had a gruff answer. " Sure, son; you walk back down and hide in that chaparral at the mouth of the canyon. When you see Cody Younger and his crew comin', you let the rest of us know. With more luck than we probably deserve, we just might be able to shoot one off his horse and get you that carbine."

John walked away. Conner handed Frank the reins to his mount and also walked off, but in the opposite direction. He reached the base of that broad, dusty trail and started up it. If Menard or Neilon were anywhere close by he would at least be able to spot their dust from the overhead plateau, and right now he desperately needed those men. He had no illusions at all about what Younger would attempt if nightfall forced Neilon and Menard to stop

E

searching. Younger would then have about eight hours to find Conner and the Parkers, stalk them in their hidden place, and eliminate them by starshine before they could do much about it.

The trail wasn't steep, particularly, but it took a lot of unaccustomed leg-work to reach the top of it, and Sheriff Conner like all true horsemen, wasn't much of a walker. He stopped three times, the last time while he was close to the top-out. Below, Frank and his father stood by the spring watching him. They looked less than half-size down there. Farther along, where the thick brush choked their canyon's mouth, he could scarcely discern John Parker's back and legs in the chaparral thicket. John was the most vulnerable of them all; he had no gun at all, not even a hand-gun.

Conner covered the last hundred yards and stepped upon the broad plateau where only a very few old oaks broke up an immense northward flow of curing grass upon a plain which was nearly flat for at least three miles. If there had been any horsemen out there, even though dusk was fast settling now, he'd have spotted their movement. Nothing moved. His heart sank a little. He stood for a while looking in all directions feeling mildly irritated. How could Al and Bert, with their combined crews of rangeriders, be so difficult to locate in this country where they had to be?

He went back down to the trail, cast a final, desperate look all around, then plunged along at a swift trot towards the bottom of their hiding place once more. The horses had been hobbled and set free, bridles hanging from saddle-horns, cinchas loosened. Frank and Jeb saw in Conner's face long before the sheriff got close that he'd found no source of succour up above. Jeb held up his little derringer. Here, under these drastically altered conditions, that deadly little weapon looked ridiculously like a toy. Jeb made a wry face.

"Sure got to get close to 'em now," he said dryly. "An' I only got one load left—it's in the underneath chamber."

Frank and Jim Conner had the sixguns. They also had ample ammunition in their belt-loops. But as Jeb had just pointed out respecting his little belly-gun, short-guns weren't much use against carbines.

"It'll get dark soon," said Jim, eyeing their overhead patch of steely sky. "After that I reckon we'd better get out of here and head on around to the east and try to make it as far as the stageroad. From there we can get back to Lincoln."

Old Jeb's furry brows shot straight up. "Lincoln? Well now, Sheriff, I'll sure agree we need better armament, only I sort of hate goin' that far out of the way to get it. Ain't there a ranch close by?"

"Southward," said Jim, eyeing the Parkers caustically. "Straight southward right past Cody Younger and his riders—who happen to have all the firepower and long-range utensils they need to prevent us from gettin' very far down-country."

Jim went to the pool, got belly-down to drink and wash his face, sat up and looked around. John was walking back up towards him from the lower end of their hiding place. John was grave; Conner couldn't recall off-hand ever seeing the younger Parker smile.

"See or hear anything?" asked Jim, straightening up to his full height.

John shook his head. "Quiet as a tomb out there. They either went back to the cave or they've scattered out trying to find us by sight. It's too shadowy out there now to track

us here. In another half hour it'll be too dark even to see
one another."

Frank and his father strolled over to hear what John had
to say, then the four of them sat upon the grass near the
spring. Three of them made smokes. The fourth one, gazing
up towards the failing light along the yonder trail, asked
what lay above. Jim Conner explained about the plateau
and what he thought they should do as soon as it got dark
enough. John listened gravely, then wordlessly arose and
strolled back down where he could keep watch upon the
southward broken country.

His father spoke, softly, eyeing the retreating form of his
youngest son. " I reckon in a show-down, that one'd have
the best brains of us all." Jeb turned inquiringly and Frank
nodded agreement. There wasn't the slightest hint of
jealousy.

An old uneasiness returned to mildly annoy Conner.
Elizabeth Parker was still alone over at the Menard place.
He partly blamed himself for that, partly blamed Al for not
thinking of it when Jim had neglected to. He mentioned it
and Jeb pondered a moment, finally saying, " Those carbines we need; why not head for the Menard place to get
'em instead of goin' all the way back to town, Sheriff?"

It was a sound idea. Conner nodded. " Al'll have extra
guns," he agreed, arising to his full height. " All right, boys;
I reckon it's dark enough now to try for it. You ready?"

They were. Jeb and Jim Conner went after the horses
while Frank sauntered down to get his younger brother.

CHAPTER SIXTEEN

THEY LEFT their hiding place by simply riding up out of it at the north end. Up there the night didn't appear as deep and gloomy as it had down below. But, although that little scimitar-moon was up there in its purple world of diamond-points as it had been the night before, unchanged at least to the naked eye, for some reason the night appeared to be somewhat brighter.

Sheriff Conner led off easterly with the land lifting some-what beneath the hooves of their horses until they were on top of the massive wall of black stone which, sheared off to the southward, became down there that cliff-face where they'd had every reason to believe hours before they were to be entombed.

There was a tangy, wild fragrance to the grass and scrub at this height. There was also a rather steady little low breeze blowing out of the invisible north. Conner halted often, listening, looking about, feeling the pulse of the night. As he commented to Jeb who rode stirrup with him, the possibility was excellent that even if they found Menard and Neilon, they would be fired upon by mistake.

Behind his father and Sheriff Conner, riding with his brother, Frank Parker said, " The night always favours the under-dog, Sheriff."

Jim didn't argue that point.

They got over as far as the yonder broken, haunted world of rock and brush and stunted trees where a skein of blind canyons like crooked fingers, indicated the eastward extent of the cliff-face and its overhead plateau. This was the area where they'd been taken off by Walsh and the 'breed cowboy.

There was not much chance of encountering any of Younger's riders over here; at least Jim didn't think there was. All the same they went warily, halting frequently and scouting ahead singly from time to time.

Then a horse softly blew its nose below, somewhere in the dark and twisted depths of one of the broad, brushy places, and they halted together, stepped off, drew their almost useless weapons and waited, each man with a hand lying lightly upon the face of his horse, ready instantly to slip down and pinch off a similar noise, or a neigh, by their own animals.

"Scout," breathed young John. "Scout or a watcher down there in hiding some place."

His father's calm, steady reply was saturnine. "We know that much son; the question is: From Younger or those other fellers?"

John said he'd slip down there on foot and find out. Conner reached and restrained him. John was undoubtedly a good man, and he was as obviously tough-boned and muscular as either his father or brother. But this was a time when they couldn't afford any noise by an alerted sentry. Further; what they especially needed right now, was someone oaken enough to take on anyone and best them.

"You boys wait here," he told the two sons of Jeb Parker. Then he turned, beckoned to their father, and glided off north-easterly where he knew the ground tipped upwards and fell off down into the first canyon. He could have gone straight ahead to achieve the same objective, but there were no trees nor any other worthwhile cover in that direction.

Jeb was wraith-like, which Conner had rather thought he might be. There were times in life when just no substitute could be found for experience and this was one of them. Whoever he was, down there hiding and waiting, he undoubtedly had a carbine in the boot of his saddle. Youthful enthusiasm might succeed, Jim was perfectly willing to concede, but youthful enthusiasm also had a bad habit of being very impatient, and if that man down there fired off just one shot from his saddle-gun, friends as well as enemies would be alerted—providing, Conner thought dourly, any friends were still around.

They navigated the slope almost to its bottom. Where Jim halted he leaned and whispered.

" He'll be in this first canyon. That sound from his horse wasn't far enough away to come from the other ones. But . . ." Jim gave the older man's forearm a hard squeeze by the way of hard emphasis. " I'll give you odds Younger and the others will be damned close by."

Jeb had no comment to make. He was clutching his ridiculous little derringer and crouching in a listening position. Conner turned and eased forward again. The dry grass was as brittle as straw and made a faint, dry sound as they passed through it. Fortunately, near the bottom of the downhill gradient rock thrust up through, the grass ceased growing, and now an occasional black waist-high scrub-bush grew in the sterile soil. These provided fair cover. The farther into the canyon Jim and Jeb Parker crept, the thicker became this wiry brush.

Also the farther they went the darker it got for now the moon was lost to them and only starlight filtered down. In

this hushed, stygian place Jim Conner picked up the scent
of horse sweat. It was strong enough to come through the
ranker, more subtle scent of the underbrush, and to Sheriff
Conner that meant simply that the animal had to be close
by.

He squatted behind a low, thick bush and looked at Jeb
Parker. The older man had a deep-score line straight
across his leathery forehead. His questing eyes kept moving.
Evidently Jeb had also scented that horse.

Jim put out a hand to tell Parker to remain where he
was, then, easing around the bush, Conner stepped out
placing each foot tentatively down testing the ground for
twigs before bringing up the other foot. He was confident of
just one thing; that crouching spy was somewhere in the onward depth of this gloomy, brushy place.

Conner was gingerly straightening out of a crouch when
something moved ahead and to his right, over closer to
where the canyon wall fluted upwards towards the overhead plateau. There was a large brushed-off place over
there where pale, blurry light fell. The movement was repeated; slow, phlegmatic, heavy. Jim thought it had to be
the watcher's horse. He tried squatting low enough to catch
some starshine to skyline the thing against, and failed dis-
mally because of the canyon's gloom-layered wall.

He started ahead again, barely breathing, using each
arm to stabilise his infinitely slow and painful stalk. Movement came again. He halted but did not crouch. A horse
turned its long, doleful face and gravely gazed back at him.
Again Conner held his breath for a few seconds, waiting to
see whether or not the horse would snort or otherwise show
alarm and perhaps warn his master, who also had to be
close by.

The horse did nothing; he simply looked, then looked

away. Conner's breath quietly ran out. He palmed the six-gun he'd taken from Wally Walsh, took several more mincing, silent steps ahead, halted to ease down very low to see through and around some chaparral, picked out patches of a smoke-tanned rider's vest, and had the answer to half his problem. He now knew where the man's horse and also, more important, where the man was.

What he didn't know was which side the man might be on, but he had no intention of taking any chances whatsoever. He briefly considered going back to bring Jeb on up in case he needed support, but abandoned this immediately because two men simply could not retrace Conner's steps without making some noise.

He remained silent for a while, deeply breathing and figuring out which way the man was hunkering, which would be his right-hand side, and how close Jim had to get himself, before he could try a launching spring over the top of that flourishing bush at the man's back to land squarely atop him.

An owl hooted across the canyon. It could have been a signal or it could have been a legitimate cry, Jim didn't know. He decided to assume it was an owl and got down on all fours to cover the last fifty feet, after which he raised up, saw his adversary just across the same squatty chaparral bush, and sprang up, launching himself over the top of the thing just as the watcher cupped both hands and made an owl cry!

It was too late. Jim knew it in the fleeting seconds before his body came down across the bush and hit that caller, knocking the man violently forwards and ending his all's-well answering hoot in a ragged loud gasp. That hadn't been a real owl across the canyon!

The cowboy somehow escaped having the wind knocked

out of him which had been Conner's intention, and kicked
savagely with his right foot at the lawman's dark shadow.
Conner knew, even as he lunged hard for the stranger's
right hand, that his friend over across the canyon would
now be warned and in all probability would come over to
investigate. This made Jim almost desperate in the way he
lashed out, slid his fist across the cowboy's raised forearm
and against the man's cheek with most of the force deflected by that out-flung arm.

The cowboy arched his back throwing Conner half off.
He tucked both legs beneath himself and tried to jack-knife
straight up off the ground, but Conner's weight prevented
him from more than reaching his knees. From this position,
making no attempt to draw his sixgun, the startled and
thoroughly angry rangeman threw a pounding right that
connected, making Conner blink, and followed that up
with a looping left that missed by eighteen inches.

Jim sought to lunge again, to hit the man's chest with
his shoulder to topple him backwards. Instead, he caught an
eye-watering blow under the ear that made him grab and
desperately hang on. This was no Wally Walsh, whoever he
was; this was a man whose reflexes bounced right back
even before he knew why he'd been assaulted from behind
like that.

Jim tried grabbing the rangeman's middle, but the cowboy swerved making him miss with one hand. The other
hand however had leather and cloth in it. Jim threw himself backwards to wrench his adversary off-balance forward,
and this time he succeeded. But as the stranger came forward, he aimed another of those sledge-hammer rights.
However, Jim saw this one being fired and ducked under it.
Then he released his adversary, jumped up panting, and
was ready when the rangeman also came uncoiled up off

the ground. Jim was mad all the way down to the soles of his feet. He breathed a curse and sprang in, lashing with his left to paw the other man off balance, stepping left and right to heighten this objective, then, when he saw the opening, he fired his right fist.

It sounded like someone breaking an oak limb across stone. The cowboy's feet left the ground, his hat sailed off through the darkness, and he fell backwards without making any attempt to break his fall. That squatty, thick bush behind them caught his dead weight, broke the fall and let him down easily.

Someone was coming fast, unmindful of how much noise he made, up through the lower-down chaparral from across the canyon. Jim whirled, saw no one, jumped away and hastened over beside the unconscious man's horse grabbing for the booted carbine as he swept on by. At least they now had a carbine, which at least was something for all the straining effort.

A man's hard curses hissed through the rearward night. Evidently that oncoming rangerider had found the man Jim Conner had just belted senseless. Using a precautionary measure, Conner dropped to one knee behind a bush and remained perfectly motionless. He half expected that other one back there to whirl and rake the nearby underbrush with gunfire, but it didn't happen. At least right then it didn't happen.

He jumped up and zigzagged his way back where Jeb was poised to move out one way or the other at once. He handed Jeb the carbine, paused to breathe deeply for a moment, then jerked his head and without a word started back up the slope the same way they'd reached the canyon's floor.

They got half way up and were stopped, panting, when

from below and southward someone fired a carbine. The bullet ploughed up flinty grit a hundred feet in front of them. The man was shooting uphill, hard under the best circumstances, but in the darkness he'd underestimated his range even more. But he'd skylined them; they knew that as soon as they ran on again, crouching over to minimise a repetition as best they could, and still make haste.

Over where this second enemy had been earlier, across the canyon, all hell broke loose; carbines pumped slugs up the slope without a stop until Jim called on Jeb to flatten out until the volley-firing was over with. He wasn't afraid of being seen and hit, he was fearful of running into a wild shot. He knew Younger and his remaining men across the canyon couldn't actually see either of them, but they'd commenced firing on the strength of that other man's shot.

Jeb winced as a bullet hit rock ten feet to his left with a sodden, tearing sound. He turned a grey set of features towards Jim and grimaced. He was clutching that carbine as though his entire future existence depended upon it.

Eventually the gunfire slackened, then died out altogether. Jim jumped up and sprinted hard for a hundred yards on up the slope before he had to drop flat gulping for breath again. Jeb was slower getting up there, but he wasn't breathing as hard when he finally arrived. They were less than twenty yards from the top-out, and made those last few yards with pumping lungs and dragging feet.

Young John and his brother were up there, tense as coiled springs, holding their horses and straining to see what was happening in the stygian darkness down below.

As Conner lunged for his horse he said, " Let's get to hell out of here, boys, your paw an' I stumbled into the whole passel of them!"

Everyone clambered aboard. Conner skirted straight

northward to get around the upper end of that perilous canyon, then eased his horse easterly again. Eventually he meant to drop southward towards the Menard place, but for as long as he figured there was a good chance of re-encountering Younger's men, he kept loping due east.

The only sound, after a while when they halted to listen, was the hard breathing of the two older men. Jeb kneed his mount up and held out the carbine. Jim took it, looked around for John, and tossed the thing to him with a wry exclamation.

" Happy birthday!"

They struck out for the last time heading due eastward and didn't stop their horses again until they were a long three miles from the depths of that deadly canyon. Then, slowing to a fast walk, Sheriff Conner struck out southward, straight for the Menard ranch.

He was bruised and scratched, and had a world of respect for the fists of that man he'd eventually knocked out back there. Whoever he was; he certainly could hit hard!

CHAPTER SEVENTEEN

THEY WERE being paralleled. Jeb initially thought they were being followed but young John said those hastening horsemen out there were paralleling them and closing in a little at a time. They paused to listen and at once the other riders also halted. They ran on for a half mile, stopped again, heard what might have been their own echoes for a moment or two, then the other riders halted again, and silence came.

Frank asked Jim Conner where he thought their trail would juncture with the trail of those other nocturnal riders. Jim's answer scarcely heeded the question and didn't answer it at all. He was gazing to the west as he gave it.

"Wherever we want to meet them, Frank. It's our ball game the way they're playin' it. All we've got to do is bend more to the left, or speed up a little, and they'll do the same."

Conner proved this by altering course slightly as he loped ahead again. Obediently, the men out there a half mile or so to the west also slightly altered course. Three times this was done, but the fourth time, when Jim swerved slightly to the right which was over in the direction of their nocturnal companions, the other men stepped up their speed a little and didn't give way at all, which meant they now understood that they'd been detected and were ready to close in.

Conner hauled back, turned and headed north back the way they'd just come. He rode hard for twenty minutes, raised his arm and slid down to a halt. As soon as they could all hear the other horsemen racing after them in an effort to close the distance and get close, Jim turned, booted out his horse and headed straight southward. His idea was elemental. Running men a half mile apart in the darkness only went by sounds. He'd reversed course making their pursuers believe he was trying to flee from them, and they, realising finally what they were sure he was up to, had also come about, but then in order to close the widening gap, they'd had to ride hard without any stops to catch up. Meanwhile, riding just as hard southward, and far enough away so that his hoof-falls wouldn't be noticed when the two parties passed in the night, Sheriff Conner led his companions in a bee-line for the Menard place.

He didn't halt until he was close enough to the ranch to make the final run in one rush. Jeb, ear cocked, spat and grinned and waggled his head. " Good thinkin'," he said to Jim Conner. " You sure out-Indianed 'em. How much farther to the ranch?"

" We're there," said Conner, lifting his reins and leading them through the final stretch of intervening night.

Menard's buildings were dark, silent, and somehow ominous. A powerful urge towards caution rose up in Sheriff Conner. He took them over into a bosque of cottonwoods a short distance out, and there the four of them left the horses.

John had the carbine. Conner and Frank Parker had six-guns. Jeb still had only that little belly-gun. The others looked at him and Jeb shrugged. It couldn't be helped so he'd live with it until the condition could be rectified.

Conner led off again, taking them on foot around towards the back of the main house. No one made a sound; from the ranchyard an equal depth of silence came out to them in dark waves of menace.

Conner was certain of two things: One; they couldn't waste a whole lot of time here. Two; those men who'd pursued them would by now have halted up north somewhere and would be angrily figuring out that they'd been made fools of. They'd probably head southward again. Jim had no doubt at all that Cody Younger was leading those men. It would have been a fairly easy thing for Younger to lead his gun-crew up out of that canyon where they'd been hiding, because the best way out was to the east, and that was exactly where Conner and the Parkers had first heard their pursuers.

Frank came up even with Jim and pointed towards the

back of the house. There was a shotgun barrel lying across a sill over there. They all halted to consider this phenomenon. What struck all of them as odd was the fact that although they'd strode directly across in front of the gun and were now beyond it, no one had swung the weapon to keep them covered.

"Dummy," whispered Frank. "Meant to scare someone off."

Jeb said to his sons, "Your sister's in there. If she's alone we're all right."

Young John grunted dourly about that. "We'd look just like anyone else to her in this darkness. You fellers stay here. I'll sneak on up and let her know who it is and what we want here."

Jim Conner said nothing as the youngest Parker slipped ahead approaching that shotgun at an angle. Jim's personal conviction was that there was no one behind that shotgun, but right then this didn't worry him as much as those men who'd chased them worried him. He listened hard but heard nothing. Jeb did the same. But it was Frank who said, "If they came on slow and tied up out beyond the buildings somewhere, we likely wouldn't hear 'em anyway."

That was quite true. Still, Conner, because for the time being he had nothing else to do, kept concentrating on picking up some kind of a sound out there in the northward night.

A night-bird drowsily called. Jeb tipped up his head and made an even better imitation; Jeb made his call sound as though the night-bird farther out was sleepily disgruntled at being awakened. The drowsy bird called one more time and Jeb nodded.

"It's John. Everything's all right. Let's go, Sheriff."

Conner headed over towards the back door of Menard's house. He walked warily even yet, but when he saw John and his sister standing in darkness near the rear wall, Conner abandoned his caution and moved up swiftly. Elizabeth went at once to her father, she'd obviously been frightened, staying alone in those dark rooms.

Sheriff Conner knew the interior of Menard's house well enough to pass straight on through the pantry, the parlour, the kitchen, and head for the east-west hallway where the gunrack hung upon a long expanse of undecorated wall. Frank came with him but young John and Jeb remained for a moment in the kitchen with Elizabeth.

There were six carbines and four sixguns in the wall-rack. Frank and Jim Conner helped themselves to carbines. Frank took two of the sixguns, one for his father, one for his younger brother, then he picked out a carbine for Jeb too, and went out into the parlour where the others were coming through.

After everyone was adequately armed Jim Conner left the Parkers inside whispering back and forth, and slipped out front to gauge the night. This time he definitely heard the low, muffled sound of riders approaching. His estimate was that they were still perhaps a mile off, but they weren't walking their horses, they were coming on in a slow lope. He stepped to the doorway and softly called.

Jeb and Frank came at once. John came later, with an arm around his sister. They all heard the sound. Jeb swore a mild oath and said Younger sure was dogged. He also said if he'd been in Cody Younger's boots he wouldn't be bothering with revenge, he'd be making tracks out of the Nebraska territory as fast as a horse could carry him.

Sheriff Conner had an answer to that. " I don't think Younger really believes his world's falling down around him. He's got too big an ego for that. He still figures that if he can eliminate us, and probably Carl down in the town jailhouse, he still can bail himself out of trouble."

No one commented after Conner made that statement. Probably because the Parkers knew how towering Younger's conceit was without talking about it.

John stepped back inside with his sister. Frank followed them but the pair of older men remained out upon the night-scented porch of Al Menard's house, listening, thinking, and speculating on the outcome, if they were attacked inside the house.

"Good odds now," grunted Jeb, finally. "Plenty of guns and ammunition and some pretty thick walls to turn their bullets, Sheriff."

Conner agreed with all this in silence. What still perplexed him was that Neilon and Menard, with their riders, hadn't shown up to lend a hand at all throughout this long night and the preceding late afternoon. They'd surely heard the gunfire beyond the cave, and later, the other gunfire down in the canyon eastward of the cliff-face. All Jim could come up with was that he and the Parkers had been moving too fast and too often for Al and Bert to catch up. Parker said something, then, which showed that he was also wondering about this.

"Those friends of yours must've got lost in the darkness, Sheriff. Maybe they're back where we were but haven't figured out where we went from there."

Jim said, "Yeah, maybe. Now listen. You can't hear anything. That means Younger's walking his horses. If he heads for the same bosque of trees where we left our animals . . ."

"Yeah," murmured Jeb dryly. "Well; he'll find out we're here soon enough. If he sets the horses loose it won't make any difference to us, Sheriff. I figure we've run just about as far as we can."

A coyote barked to the north-west. Another coyote answered it over to the north-east of the yard. Conner sneered. "Lousy imitation. They should've stuck to that owl call."

Jeb eased back deeper into the porch shadows and carefully examined the carbine he'd appropriated from Al Menard's stock of weapons. It was clean, lightly oiled and loaded. He said, "Sheriff; you better move back. There's starshine out there in the yard."

Jim obeyed, then he dropped to one knee, using his carbine as a staff to lean upon. When Jeb followed suit the coyotes barked again, closer together now, as though one of Younger's men had been scouting on ahead and had halted after the first call to await the arrival of his companions.

"Be a right good time for those friends of yours to show up, about now," muttered Jeb.

Conner said nothing. He wasn't relying on any outside help. The day before he'd thought Menard and Neilon would catch up, but during the long, deadly night he'd come to rely only upon himself and his companions. Now, more than ever, he doubted that Menard and Neilon would get up in time to lend a hand in the coming fight. But it didn't worry him. The odds, as near as he could figure them, were pretty close to even, for even if Walsh and that other rangerider Conner had belted senseless were along, recovered and ready to fight again, he still didn't believe Cody had enough men to off-set the thick walls of Menard's house, which were on the side of the law and the law's friends.

And yet Conner had a little chilly feeling in the pit of his stomach. Cody Younger had made his living with his wits, not guns. That kind of a man was infinitely more dangerous as an enemy than some quick-draw killer who only thought in terms of muzzleblast.

The coyotes were silent now. Out across the yard there was nothing to be seen nor heard for a long while. The overhead sky kept turning steadily darker. The little stingy moon was far down, the stars also seemed to be retreating at a great rate of speed. Shadows stood out darker around the buildings than in the expanse of empty yard. Behind Conner and Jeb Parker the house door stood ajar. Frank leaned back there and over on Frank Parker's right his younger brother was standing motionless by a window.

An owl hooted. Conner got the direction right away and let his breath slowly run out. It had come from that bosque of trees where they'd left their horses. Younger knew now for a fact where his enemies were.

Jeb turned his head and softly spoke to Frank. " One of you go through to the back rooms an' keep watch out there."

Frank wordlessly faded out into the gloomy staleness of the house. John didn't move away from his window but Betty came over to stand behind her father where Frank had been. Jeb muttered for her to go into the kitchen, which was on the east end of the house, and keep watch there. He also said she ought to take a weapon with her.

John turned from his window and without saying a word passed through towards the west end of the house. Jim Conner heard the younger man walking over wooden floors and grimly inclined his head; no one had to tell that one what to do nor where to go.

The owl hooted mournfully again, this time out behind Al Menard's mighty log barn. They were beginning to sneak up, to close in. Jim turned his head. He and Jeb exchanged a knowing look. From now on there would be no more running.

Conner arose, jerked his head and stepped back inside. He eased the door closed, set the bar from the inside which locked it, and sauntered over to join Jeb at the window where John Parker had been.

"A little moonlight would've helped," muttered Jeb.

"If they get much closer," growled Jim, "you'll have all the light you need. They'll set fire to this damned house."

Jeb nodded. "Nice thought, Sheriff."

They didn't hear the owl again. In fact for the next ten minutes they didn't hear anything at all. As always, it was the waiting that sapped a man. To pass time Jeb made a cigarette and stuck it between his lips without lighting it. Sheriff Conner examined his shooting-iron for the second time and strolled through the house making certain everyone was on watch. They were. He visited little Elizabeth last. She looked up at him in the gloom with eyes as large as silver dollars. He smiled and laid a hand lightly upon her shoulder. "If your husband could see you now he'd sure be proud, little lady."

She was candid in her answer to that. "Sheriff; if my husband were here I'd feel a lot braver." She made a wan little grin.

Conner returned to the front parlour and told Betty's father what she'd said. Jeb's lips lifted slightly in a ghostly smile but his eyes didn't laugh at all. He pointed. "Keep an eye on the front of the barn. I think I caught a shadow down there."

Conner was just bending to look when the bluish blast of a carbine down there lanced the night. The window in front of Conner exploded into a thousand pieces and Jeb

Parker dropped his carbine with both hands up in front of his face as he stumbled backwards in a crippled way.

Jim pushed out his gun and shot back, but the rifleman down there at the barn had jumped away the moment he'd fired. Jim then turned to go help Jeb into a chair. Blood was running under Parker's hands. Flying glass had cut him badly, it seemed.

CHAPTER EIGHTEEN

THAT GUNSHOT from the front of Menard's barn was the signal. All hell broke loose. Younger and his men had been out there some little time. They'd been skulking around to get into the best positions for raking the house, which they proceeded to do after that initial shot had shattered the parlour window.

Sheriff Conner heard the remaining windows quiver from gunshots, both inside and outside, as he stepped into the kitchen, grabbed a dish towel, plunged it into a bucket of drinking water and swiftly returned to Jeb Parker's side. While the first savage exchange was still under way he forced Jeb's hands down and bent close.

Flying slivers of glass had cut Parker's chin, both cheeks and slit the lobe of one ear, but Jeb must have been tilting his head downward, because the low brim of his hat had saved both eyes. He didn't have any cuts higher than the bridge of his nose. Still though, the blood made it appear that he'd been nearly killed. As soon as Sheriff Conner was sure Parker's eyes were all right, he pressed the wet rag into

Jeb's hands, grabbed up his carbine and returned to the window.

In the rear of the house Frank cut loose with that shotgun Betty had hopefully lay across a sill. It made the whole house reverberate. When he let go with the second barrel it sounded even louder.

To the east there was no attack, but along the west wall which lay southward from the barn and corral area, gunmen were firing and jumping and firing again. John Parker was systematically replying. To Jim Conner, who listened, gauging the progress of the fight, it seemed that John Parker was firing less for effect than for hits. He didn't always reply to a gunshot. Other times he'd lever and tug off one shot right after another, as though he'd sighted a sprinting gunman and was trying to cut him down before he reached shelter.

The fighting seemed finally to shift somewhat, as though Younger's men decided attacking the west of the house was too dangerous. While they were shifting positions the fighting dwindled. At least the men out back and the ones to the west slackened off.

Jim was worried and turned to look back where Jeb had been. He wasn't there. Across the room the pantry door was still moving. That was what had been worrying Sheriff Conner, but if Jeb had gone into the kitchen, then they'd be safe in that direction also.

Jim faced forward again. He was dogmatically waiting for that one down inside Menard's barn to try another lucky shot. So far that was the only one of Cody's men who'd scored. Of course the gunman down there didn't know that, but Jim Conner did, and it was Jim Conner's way to want to settle his debts one at a time.

Eventually the gunman down there fired again. This

time slanting his fire to hit the north-easterly corner of the house where one kitchen window opened out upon the front yard.

Jim wasn't ready that time. But he now placed his carbine across the sill and eased down around it, steady as a rock and endlessly patient. Elsewhere, the gunfire started to brisk up again. True to Conner's guess, the attackers had left the lethal gunfire of John Parker along the west wall, and had slipped around to the east. Frank let fly with both barrels of the scattergun again, as though he'd perhaps sighted movement out back from west to east. Then Frank fired several more shots with his carbine.

The gunman down at the barn eased out. Jim saw him, settled lower, picked up the vague silhouette in his front sights and was easing back on the trigger when the gunman fired first, his bullet ripped a chunk out of the log just under Jim's window, shook the wall and when Conner fired back he missed by a good five inches. The gunman at the barn gave a big bound backwards and lit out of sight in the barn. It evidently had shocked him considerably to realise someone inside the house was making a personal duel out of this fight. He didn't return to the barn's front entrance again.

Jim swore with feeling at his missed opportunity, straightened back to eject his spent casing, and the guns over on the east side of the house opened up with a withering volley that broke glass in the kitchen, shattered chairs and plates and bounced off the mighty cast-iron stove like beads.

Jim went into the parlour, waited for a lull then jumped on through into the kitchen. The first thing to catch his attention was Elizabeth Parker's pony-tail of long hair; each time she'd yank off a carbine shot, the pony-tail would jump wildly from the recoil. He went across to her, took her arm and pulled her away into a sheltered corner.

"Stay there," he yelled at her through the gun-thunder. "I'll take your place!"

Jeb had his hands full. He had blood over his shirt-front, down across one shoulder from the slit ear-lobe, and in the wild flash of gunfire looked more dead than alive, until he turned; then Conner saw the fire-points of light in his eyes.

The two of them shot, ducked, raised up and shot again. They didn't have much ground to manoeuvre in; the entire kitchen was only about twenty by thirty feet in width and depth, which was large enough for a kitchen but hardly large enough for a pair of gunmen to stand off a savage attack.

Bullets struck all around them. They tried mightily to shoot back as soon as they saw muzzleblast. Otherwise, it was too dark out there, and the attackers had an added advantage; there were two sheds, probably for chickens, which they could jump behind after they fired. But sooner or later, if Younger's men kept this up, jumping out to fire then jumping back again, someone was going to get hit.

Someone did, only it wasn't outside, it was inside. A bullet seared like a branding iron between Sheriff Conner's right elbow and his ribs. It burned, making the lawman grunt a curse and flinch. He moved over into the sheltered place where Betty was, made a quick examination, saw that except for the ragged tear from front to back and the welling scarlet stain, he hadn't been badly injured, and went back to his window again.

He was coldly bloodthirsty now, let several gunners shoot without firing back, and bided his time. It evidently appeared to Younger and his men out there that only one defender was still able to fire from inside the kitchen because they turned a little, concentrating their shots against

Jeb's window. Parker had to eventually crouch down below the sink, unable to even hold up his carbine for random shots.

Jim straightened up very slowly and carefully, lay his weapon across the chewed up wooden sill, waited until two men jumped out, guns blazing, and squeezed off his shot. The last one of those men, who was nearest to the shed, took that bullet straight through from high up in front out the back. He didn't cry out or even shudder. He flipped his carbine with one hand, half punched backwards by impact, and fell directly into the second gunman, who was trying to push past to cover.

Jim levered up his next load, dropped his head and shot the second, frantically scrabbling man, but a post of the chicken-run slightly deflected his bullet; it hit the second man low in the leg, crumbling him to the ground where he cried out in agony and terror, and tried mightily to crawl away.

Jeb Parker sprang up, now that the confusion out there had caused a slight pause in the firing, took in the yonder scene with one sweep, threw up his carbine and fired. The second man, crawling frantically, shivered his full length, raised up to look ahead at his friends in total surprise, then he fell forward across his dead companion.

For several moments there was no more gunfire. Jim told Jeb he didn't think Cody had more than two men left, unless of course he'd been joined sometime in the night by more of his rangeriders from Younger's home-ranch.

Suddenly a savage pair of raking sixgun shots slammed into the chicken house from around back of Menard's house, on the outside. For a startled moment Jim and Jeb looked big-eyed at one another.

Jeb said : " Menard and those other men, you reckon?"

Conner waited, holding back his judgement. Finally, when that sixgun back there went silent and for five seconds there wasn't a gunshot from anywhere, Jim shook his head. "Not Al or Bert. If it was there'd be bullets coming from every direction. Just one man out there."

"Frank," breathed Jeb, whipping around and heading for the back door.

Conner caught and held on. "You go out there now and you could be killed by your own son. Stay away; go back to your window."

Jeb pulled free, but he hung back for a moment, until Elizabeth called softly, then he nodded and turned back. Outside the house it was as still as death. Sheriff Conner had a premonition about that. He took his carbine and went back out into the parlour. John was standing near the window. He and Conner exchanged a look. The younger man gave his head a little wag.

"They're up to something."

He'd scarcely gotten it out than his brother's sixgun crashed and roared from out back again, and that time even Jim Conner ran back through the pantry and kitchen towards the rear door. John was right on his heels and Jeb had preceded them both out of the house. The second Conner jumped low and to the right, beyond the doorway, gunfire erupted from over by the chicken run. Conner lit flat down and rolled twice before coming up with his carbine pushed out. Frank, Jeb and John Parker were firing straight back, driving Younger and his survivors back. Jim yelled at them to keep it up, recklessly sprang to his feet and ran hard straight across towards the farthest shed. A man over there, risking a peek out, saw him coming and yelled a wild alarm as he turned and fled. Conner fired twice. The third time his carbine hammer fell upon an expended casing. He hurled the weapon against the shed and drew his sixgun.

From down at the barn a deafening roar of shots opened up. That fleeing gunman jerked and jumped and spun, then fell and slid on his belly nearly fifteen feet before halting, riddled.

Jim had no time to speculate about that volley from the barn. There were two men sniping blindly so he covered the last twenty feet changing leads, going from left to right and in this fashion avoiding being struck. He saw one of those men—Wally Walsh—as the rangeboss boldly stepped out and fired pointblank. Conner's hat sailed away as though it had taken wing. Jim tugged off a hip-shot, cocked his sixgun and yanked again. Walsh's last shot went into the air, he was falling backwards as he pulled the trigger.

Conner didn't know until later that he was calling on Cody Younger to show himself, or that he'd cursed Younger fiercely as he finally reached the protective front wall of the chicken house. The man who later told him he'd done that also told him that if he hadn't, if Neilon and Menard down in the barn hadn't recognised his voice, they'd have cut him down too because they could only make out that he was running and shooting.

Younger tried poking his gun around and firing but he missed by five feet. He then tried edging away, getting ready to leap across the opening which separated the two little sheds, but Sheriff Conner knew that was his only escape route left, and let fly one bullet just to let Younger know he couldn't make it.

Younger then crept over to the south end of the shed, but that was where the guns of the Parkers were whittling the shed away so he had to desperately make that other attempt.

Sheriff Conner was waiting. He had no intention at all of taking Cody Younger alive. For ten seconds nothing happened. Everyone was waiting, watching, barely breathing. Conner sank to one knee. The fire alongside his raked-over ribs was burning more than ever from all that recent exertion. There was sweat dripping from Jim's chin. He ignored that too.

Younger hurled a rock towards the south end of the shed, and when it struck, diverting Jim's attention only for a fraction of a second, Younger made his wide jump. Jim fired just once, catching the larger man in mid-air. Younger cried out, lit down on both feet and fell, two-thirds of his body hidden behind the yonder shed, his legs from the knees down exposed in the ghostly night.

Conner waited. He stood up, reloaded from his shell-belt and made no immediate move to walk around there. He knew he'd connected. He also knew from long experience as a hunter—animal-hunter and manhunter—that the best way to be certain of a kill was to wait; let the wounded one bleed out.

" Hey Conner . . ." The voice was muffled and weak.

" Yeah."

" It's all right. Come on around here."

Jim did, but not the way Younger expected for him to. He walked across to the northernmost point of the other little shed, stepped around and was gazing at Cody Younger from behind. Younger was holding his cocked sixgun up with both hands, panting in his effort to hold on long enough to shoot when Jim came from down below.

Conner stepped lightly ahead twenty feet, leaned down and slapped the weakly-held gun out of Cody Younger's hands. The dying man dropped back, looked straight up, and called Jim Conner a fighting name with his last breath, then he settled lower and softly flattened out.

Jeb called. Jim answered, put up his sixgun and stood considering the dead man. He felt nothing, neither pity nor anger, nor even contempt. From over at the barn Al Menard sang out. That, finally, jarred Jim Conner back to the present. He called back, " Come on over, Al."

The men converged. Bert Neilon was there with his riders. Menard and Lem Pierce were also there, with their men. Jeb, Frank and John Parker also came over. Everyone viewed dead Cody Younger without comment. Bert Neilon said, " Jim; every time we'd find where you'd been, last night, you were long gone." Neilon sounded apologetic, or embarrassed. Conner said, " Hell, forget it, Bert." Then he looked straight at the older man. " 'You see the bill-of-sale?"

Neilon nodded and reddened. " I've apologised to Lem. I reckon there's no fool like an old one, is there?"

" No," agreed Jim Conner bluntly. " In your case there sure wasn't." Then he looked at Al. " That leaves you without a foreman again, doesn't it?"

Menard screwed up his face in a calculating expression. " Jim; walk on over to the house with me," he said, taking the sheriff's arm. As soon as they were alone he said, " I've been thinkin' the past few days . . . Now this little lady and her husband . . ."

Conner stopped and turned, his eyes softly smiling. " Sort of hoped you'd think of that by yourself," he said. " Al; the boy's never had a decent chance, an' now he inherits the Younger spread. He'll be one of the biggest cowmen in the country one of these days. But—he's still as green as grass. If you were to sort of take an interest . . ."

Menard nodded gravely. " Come on," he said, walking

on again. " Let's get Betty an' head for town. You reckon George Meany'll listen to reason?"

" If he doesn't," said Jim Conner, " I'll give him my badge and set Carl loose anyway. He'll listen, all right. He won't like it but he'll listen, as long as you'n I stand in back of the lad."

" Well," said Menard, and pushed out a hand. " How about it?"

They smiled at each other, solemnly shook, then went on over where Elizabeth was standing in the doorway watching their approach.

Lauran Paine who, under his own name and various pseudonyms has written over 900 books, was born in Duluth, Minnesota, a descendant of the Revolutionary War patriot and author, Thomas Paine. His family moved to California when he was at an early age and his apprenticeship as a Western writer came about through the years he spent in the livestock trade, rodeos, and even motion pictures where he served as an extra because of his expert horsemanship in several films starring movie cowboy Johnny Mack Brown. In the late 1930s, Paine trapped wild horses in Northern Arizona and, for a time, worked as a professional farrier. Paine came to know the Old West through the eyes of many who had been born in the previous century and he learned that Western life had been very different from the way it was portrayed on the screen. "I knew men who had killed other men," he later recalled. "But they were the exceptions. Prior to and during the Depression, people were just too busy eking out an existence to indulge in Saturday-night brawls." He served in the U.S. Navy in the Second World War and began writing for Western pulp magazines following his discharge. It is interesting to note that all of his earliest novels (written under his own name and the pseudonym Mark Carrel) were published in the British market and he soon had as strong a following in that country as in the United States. Paine's Western fiction is characterized by strong plots, authenticity, an apparently effortless ability to construct situation and character, and a preference for building his stories upon a solid foundation of historical fact. *Adobe Empire* (1956), one of his best novels, is a fictionalized account of the last twenty years in the life of trader William Bent and, in an off-trail way, has a melancholy, bittersweet texture that is not easily forgotten. *Moon Prairie* (1950), first published in the United States in 1994, is a memorable story set during the mountain man period of the frontier. In later novels such as *The Homesteaders* (1986) or *The Open Range Men* (1990), he showed that the special magic and power of his stories and characters had only matured along with his basic themes of changing times, changing attitudes, learning from experience, respecting nature, and the yearning for a simpler, more moderate way of life. His most recent Western novels include *Tears of the Heart*, *Lockwood* and *The White Bird*.